Bianca got to her feet, her eyes blazing

Blue eyes met furious amber yellow and held them. Then she found that she was breathing too fast, and suddenly felt a little unnerved. This couldn't be her, caught up in a situation like this.

"But I don't think I can let you go, Miss James. Not quite yet," Caspar was saying quietly. "I have to make some inquiries." His eyes still on hers, he reached behind him to where her handbag lay on the table and snapped it open. Before she realized his intention, he had extracted the passport she'd slipped into the top. Quickly, she tried to snatch it back, but he whipped it out of her reach.

"Insurance," he announced calmly. "There's not much point in your leaving here while I've got this."

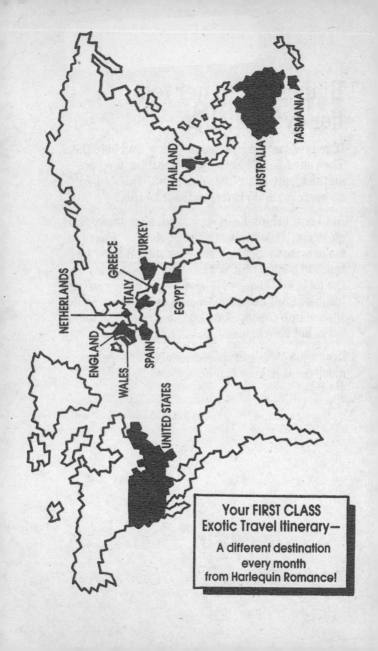

TASMANIA
AUSTRALIA
THAILAND
TURKEY
GREECE
NETHERLANDS
ITALY
EGYPT
ENGLAND
SPAIN
WALES
UNITED STATES

Your FIRST CLASS
Exotic Travel Itinerary—

A different destination
every month
from Harlequin Romance!

FALSE IMPRESSIONS
Lucy Keane

Harlequin Books

TORONTO • NEW YORK • LONDON
AMSTERDAM • PARIS • SYDNEY • HAMBURG
STOCKHOLM • ATHENS • TOKYO • MILAN

Original hardcover edition published in 1990
by Mills & Boon Limited

ISBN 0-373-03136-X

Harlequin Romance first edition July 1991

FALSE IMPRESSIONS

CHAPTER ONE

'*CRETINO! BASTARDO!*' The woman's voice rose to a window-shattering shriek. 'You think you can treat me like dirt and that I'll always come back, don't you? *Don't you*? Arrogant, selfish *bastardo!*' Then a man's voice replied, too low for Bianca to catch what was said. Heavens, she really was eavesdropping now!

But the door had been open, and it wasn't her fault if she could understand Italian. She looked at the street number again. Then she checked the typed card in her hand: Apartment No. Seven, Third Floor, Piazza della Robbia. The name in the little illuminated plate by the bell said 'Reissman'. It was where she was meant to be, at exactly the time Frieda should have arranged by phone from London—assuming, of course, that Frieda had got herself sufficiently organised to phone in the first place.

Bianca ducked instinctively as something hurtled past her head, hit the wall opposite and fell on the floor. It was a woman's shoe. If the man in there was the famous portrait painter she'd come to see, then this wasn't the ideal moment to embark on the delicate matter she had to discuss with him.

It was so unfair! Here she was, for the very first time—and purely the result of a lucky combination of circumstances—entrusted by the Antoniou Gallery with a really important job to do, the kind of job that would impress Hugh if she carried it through successfully. And what was happening? A full-scale row in the flat of the man she'd come to meet, between a pair of lovers so uninhibited in their mutual commentary that the entire piazza must be blushing by now.

She hesitated. It would be very inconvenient to have to come back. She'd arranged to be at the dealer's with

the Matisse by four o'clock, and the paintings were heavy
to cart about all over Florence. There were stories of art
thefts and muggings almost daily. Someone might grab
them in the street—her constant nightmare ever since she
had picked them up from the airport at Milan—and
Antoniou's would never trust her again.

Perhaps ringing the bell might bring them to their
senses. She could at least leave the painting for Reissman.

She pushed the button with a deceptive firmness. She
was wondering if she shouldn't just turn tail and flee. The
discreet, muted buzz was either inaudible above the
shouts, or merely ignored. The woman was crying now—
well, half crying, half screaming. It all sounded more and
more like some third-rate television 'soap'.

'I hate you! You're a pig—you don't care for anyone's
feelings except your own.'

Even a non-Italian speaker could have followed the
gist of those remarks. Then the woman gave another yell
of rage, and something else came flying through the door.

Clutching her two paintings protectively, Bianca
examined the missile as the shapeless bundle hit the
floor and spilled into a pair of men's trousers. Help! What
on earth were they doing in there? She'd *better* go.

At that moment the woman stormed past her, turning
to shout abuse as she reached the hall. She scarcely gave
Bianca a second glance in her fury, but the latter had
plenty of time to get a good impression of *her*: in her
twenties and stylishly dressed, with a very good figure—
much more bust and hip than Bianca herself could boast
of, and a narrow waist. She was tanned and well made-up,
with smooth skin and a mane of dark, hennaed hair. The
dye had coloured the ends and given it a reddish-ginger
sheen. There were natural reddish lights in Bianca's own
dark hair, but they were rather more discreet. The woman
was wearing one shoe.

'*Bastardo*!' she yelled again, picked up the shoe from
the floor, and hurled it back through the open doorway.
Flinging a passing comment at Bianca, which roughly
translated as 'If it's the selfish pig in there you want, good

luck to you!' she hopped furiously round a bend in the stairs of the old apartment block, and disappeared.

A man appeared at the door. He was barefoot—in February!—and dressed in a pair of shapeless cotton trousers, baggy at the knees, and a paint-smeared sweatshirt. He reminded Bianca instantly of some macho American film star—he should have had a gun, or a liquor bottle in his hand—except that as a sex symbol he definitely wasn't her type.

Bianca was opening her mouth to speak, but he thrust her roughly out of the way—'Just a minute!'—and, as she fell against the wall with a gasp, he strode to the staircase and hung round the banisters, shouting into the invisible depths, 'That's *it*, Monica! The last ditch—the final straw—the absolute bloody ultimate experience! Don't ever come back!'

An unintelligible and shrewish yell was the only reply.

Bianca quickly assessed her chances of making an escape before he—whoever he was—turned on her, too. But there was nowhere to run.

Then the man swung round, unexpectedly grinned at her, and approached in a couple of strides. He was taller than she'd thought at first, and he had blue eyes. Very blue.

'Sorry about that,' he said, with a casualness that took her aback after all the impassioned abuse she'd overheard. 'You wanted to see me? Come in.'

'I ... well ... *Mr Reissman*?'

There was a moment's appalled silence. Good lord. This *was* the man with whom whe was supposed to be entering into the most tactful and delicate negotiations .. . While she struggled desperately for something polite to say, she had visions of herself being flung out like Monica, and subsequently losing her job.

Then, aware that she was staring, she faltered, 'Perhaps it might be better if I came back later?' Everyone knew artists were supposed to be eccentric, but this was all the clichés rolled into one!

He gave a shrug, and another unexpected grin.

'Now's fine by me,' he said. 'Come in.' It was difficult
to believe that, only seconds before, he had been shouting
fit to raise the roof.

A doubtful nod was all she could manage in reply.

As he shepherded her into the flat, still clutching her
paintings as though they were her only contact with
reality, she was struck again by his appearance.

He was younger than she'd been led to expect,
thirty-two, thirty-three perhaps, but the most startling
thing about him was those eyes: they were almost
angelic—the sparkling, baby blue colour of perfect
innocence . . . and after the way she'd just heard him
shouting at his mistress! And he had the longest lashes
she'd ever seen—pure gold. But there the resemblance to
a heavenly being ended very firmly. His tow-coloured
hair stood out from his head at untidy angles and was
full of dust, and there was nothing at all soft about the
line of his jaw, or that aggressively squared, unshaven
chin and long, determined mouth.

The second thing that struck her was the appearance
of the flat. Once inside the door, she gasped aloud. It
looked as though a hurricane had swept through it. How
could he ever find a paintbrush in such a catastrophic
mess? Tidy and organised by endeavour if not by nature,
Bianca was genuinely shocked by the chaos in which
another human being could bring himself to live.

Suddenly there was a shout from outside, and before
she had time to pick a path through the tumble of books,
papers, clothing and cushions, he had pushed past her,
leaping with agility that argued long practice across the
confusion to the open french windows.

'Hang on a minute——'

Was that instruction intended for her—or for whoever
it was outside in the square? Perhaps this was all just a
confused dream, and she had fallen asleep still on the
plane.

There was a narrow balcony, only wide enough for a
chair if no one sat on it, with an array of pot plants
attached to the iron balustrade. Reissman—if it was

indeed he—hung over it, shouting in Italian again. She saw him deliberately pick up one of the pots, containing a flourishing begonia, and drop it. The smash was horrible, as was the scream from below. Had he injured someone?

There were louder shouts now from different parts of the old piazza, with its four-storey apartments and rusty iron balconies.

'*Va bene, va bene*!' she heard him call soothingly across to someone. 'It's OK.'

What did he mean, OK? Surely this wasn't the day-to-day routine of a successful painter? She felt sorry for the other piazza-dwellers if it were.

She stood in the wrecked room, clutching the two carefully wrapped canvases she had brought from England. It was difficult to find anywhere even to put her feet.

Her responsibilities overwhelmed her. What would be her best plan? To leave immediately, and go on to the dealer's to deliver the Matisse? There she could collect a portfolio. She could then make for the hotel where she could deposit that, and Reissman's painting, in the safe. Then, tomorrow, she could negotiate a calmer meeting with this madman over the telephone. It would mean, of course, that the business part of her visit couldn't be completed before Saturday, and she would have to spend some of her precious weekend on it. Still, the alternative, which was failure to persuade Reissman to do what the Gallery wanted, would be awful. Antoniou's would never trust her to handle any more assignments worth having.

She pushed to the back of her mind the niggling doubt Hugh had sown a few weeks ago, when she had heard that she was to have her first working trip to Florence.

'It doesn't sound like much of a ball to me,' he had remarked coolly when she'd announced the assignment to him, glowing with pride. 'I'd watch out for your Mr Geller if I were you, Bianca. You're in a no-win situation there, and he knows it. Don't tell me that any painter with the reputation of Reissman wants to be told his portrait's not good enough! Geller's set you up for a fall, so he can step in when you've made the inevitable mess of it, and pick up the pieces. He can afford to be magnanimous once he comes out of it better than you.'

'That might be the way people in banks work,' she had retorted, rising to the defence of her boss, 'especially in the nasty back-stabbing world of high finance. But Antoniou's is a small, friendly, respectable gallery and we don't do things like that to each other!'

'That's what you think!' Hugh had teased, in his cool, patronising way, and then kissed her on the end of her small straight nose.

'Not what I think—what I *know*,' she had stated firmly. But he had sown the seed of doubt, and that doubt had been secretly germinating ever since.

No, failure was out of the question. Especially as she now had something to prove to Hugh since that mix-up over the dinner party they had been giving. She was still sure she had told him she had to go to a private view that night, and that she wouldn't be able to cook for him, or act as hostess as she usually did. They hadn't had a row exactly—just a rather cold difference of opinion—but she knew he hadn't really forgiven her yet. If there was one thing Hugh hated, it was inefficiency.

So outwardly she would deal with this whole thing calmly and quietly, even if inwardly she was full of doubts about her ability to handle such a tricky negotiation. And even her mother hadn't helped. She had burst out laughing at the news. 'Bibi, darling! Poor Mr Geller ... you're the last person to send on a diplomatic mission—you're far too impulsive! Hold your tongue and count to fifty before you say anything.'

Well. She'd show her mother and Hugh she could be diplomatic and efficient. She'd fly back home on Sunday night one-hundred-per-cent successful, even if it did mean sacrificing the whole of Saturday's leisurely exploration of the Uffizi.

She'd go straight on to the dealer's now, before that madman came back.

But, before she could get anywhere near the door, both paintings were seized from her grasp and flung on to the cluttered sofa, and with a squawk of protest she was being dragged by the hand towards the window. Help! Was she going to follow the path of the begonias?

She tried to protest but, before she could utter a coherent word, she was pulled on to the balcony and clasped in the madman's arms, her nose buried in a paint-smeared sweatshirt somewhere on a level with his chest.

A vituperative exchange was taking place over her head with the invisible Monica outside in the piazza.

'What's your name?' the madman demanded suddenly, jerking her head back none too gently by her long hair.

'Bianca, but——' Her nose was thrust into the shirt again, and kept there by the pressure of a large, strong hand on the back of her head. The sweatshirt smelled of linseed oil.

There was another shouted insult, and an angry counterpoint from other apartment-dwellers. But before she could kick his shins, or bite his chest, or even draw breath to scream for help—all of which occurred to her just too late—she found her head being dragged back again. He yelled, 'È Bianca—siamo fidanzati!' and then his mouth closed on hers and she was in a clinch that wasn't a bad imitation of a passionate scene from a 1920s movie—except that as far as Mr Reissman's part in it was concerned it was for real. He was obviously not a man to waste his opportunities.

Although the whole thing had come about rather violently and he was holding her tightly, the gentleness of his mouth on hers took her by surprise. In reality, the kiss was quite brief, but to Bianca it seemed to go on and on, her body reacting independently from her mind. She was too stunned at first to register anything apart from the fact it was happening, but under the teasing persuasion of his tongue instinct had almost caused her to part her lips, when something hit a window on the floor below them—the crashing glass provoked a howl that was not Monica's.

Bianca, gasping for breath, was released instantly.

'Bloody hell,' muttered the madman. 'She's done it this time.' And, leaving Bianca to totter back against the side wall of the balcony, he leaped nimbly back into the chaos of the apartment and made for the door.

She took a deep breath.

She had recovered her wits.

How *dared* he behave in that appalling manner! Who the hell did he think he was, kissing her like that? Her own shame in responding even minimally to what he had just done fuelled her anger. Deliberately she adjusted the ivory combs that held back her long dark hair. Then she smoothed her skirt, and pulled down her jacket. She was actually shaking with rage.

She stalked back into the sitting-room, and picked her way round the obstacles. There was an impressive fur coat lying on the sofa, along with a couple of pillows and a bundled-up duvet. And several magazines. And a scattered heap of papers. And several other items of clothing. The man lived in a pigsty!

Where had he flung down the paintings? And where was her handbag? She must have let go of it when he grabbed her. If this was what working for Antoniou's was all about, they wouldn't get the chance to sack her—she'd be writing out her notice before she'd even touched down at Heathrow on Sunday night.

She found the paintings, but wasn't sure which was which. They were almost identical in size and shape, and both covered with the same protective wrappings, their seals too heavily overstamped to be legible to her. Frieda had said Reissman's painting was slightly larger, but she could hardly tell. She found her handbag, too.

The madman walked back into the room, shutting the door behind him. He had a shoe in his hand.

'Sorry about that,' he said casually, and gave her a grin that infuriated her still further. He retrieved the second shoe from the floor, and the fur coat from the sofa. Then he flung the shoes, and the coat, out over the balcony, and shut the french windows. And then he turned to face her, hands resting on narrow hips.

'So. A visiting Pre-Raphaelite maiden. What did you say your name was?'

Bianca tried to tell herself that she had come all the way to Florence especially to be tactful and conciliating to this man because, if he didn't agree to do as she asked, the Gallery would be in an impossible situation. She tried to tell herself to take another deep breath and count at least ten before she answered. But when she thought of the way he had virtually assaulted her, her mother's Latin temperament got the better of her father's English caution.

'What the hell did you think you were doing out there on that balcony—grabbing me like that and then telling that fishwife down in the piazza we're engaged!' she exploded. 'I've never set eyes on you before in my life, and as far as I'm concerned I never want to again! I've heard of eccentric painters, but you're not eccentric—you're insane! Is this the way you treat all your visitors?' Clutching paintings and handbag to her chest and breathing very fast, she confronted him, her eyes blazing.

There was a lengthy silence.

Then finally, to her outraged astonishment, he laughed.

'I don't usually enjoy the kissing part so much,' he said, grinning at her and clearly unaffected by her outburst. 'I got the Pre-Raphaelite bit all wrong—it must have been those long, wavy curls that put me off. You looked very Burne-Jones-like at first. All pale skin and soulful eyes.'

'What's that supposed to mean? An apology by way of a compliment?' she demanded.

'No, not really,' he said unchivalrously. 'I loathe the Pre-Raphaelites. A lot of loonies. What a way to paint women!'

The blatant manner in which he was assessing her appearance was disconcerting; he was taking in the high-heeled boots, calf-length navy skirt with its neat waisted jacket, and high-collared, frilled shirt. But she supposed he could be forgiven for calling her Pre-Raphaelite, since she was deliberately playing up the Victorian aspect of her looks, especially with the central parting in her hair.

'Definitely not Burne-Jones,' he added decisively. 'He didn't go in for yellow-eyed ladies. Can I help you?'

With a really heroic effort she bit back the retort she was about to make; there wasn't anything she could do to retrieve the situation, but she didn't have to make it any worse, whatever her personal antipathy towards him. 'I was looking for Mr Reissman,' she said, with an effort at sounding polite. She was disliking this scruffy, unorthodox individual more with each passing minute, and hoped against hope that he was in reality some disreputable cousin or hanger-on she had mistaken for the man himself.

'I am Caspar Reissman.' Her heart sank like a stone. It had been too much to hope. 'And you are . . .?'

'How do you do?' she said, as evenly as she could manage. 'I'm Bianca James from Antoniou's.'

The Gallery had several times exhibited his work and engineered commissions for him in the past, but he eyed her unhelpfully. 'Oh? I've never been honoured by a personal visit before. It must be earth-shattering news. Unless you've just dropped in for a friendly drink?'

'I have a letter for you from the Gallery,' she said shortly. 'Mr Geller's secretary hasn't managed to contact you?'

Of course she hadn't—that was more than obvious—but Bianca felt in desperate need of official backing. She was in a difficult position: she knew the moment wasn't right for what she had to say, but postponing the interview was extremely inconvenient. Would the Gallery regard it as a legitimate expense if she took him out to lunch? Not that she relished the idea of taking this appalling man anywhere unless he changed his clothes. But, once wined and dined, he might mellow into something like normality, and they could both forget about the unfortunate beginning to their interview.

His fair brows were drawn into a slight frown, under that remarkably untidy thatch of hair. 'Geller called me a few weeks ago—is that what you mean?'

'What was it about?'

He shrugged. 'Just to say that my last commission for the Gallery had arrived safely. Not a man of many words, Mr Geller.'

That was the only point so far on which she agreed with him, but she didn't say so. Her heart was beating too fast from all the extra adrenalin in her system, and her arms were beginning to ache from holding the paintings, which were heavy and awkward. She looked round for somewhere to put them down. She was feeling more and more at a disadvantage; her businesslike manner was half pretence at the best of times anyway, and now any belief she had had in her ability to handle the situation was evaporating fast. Hugh had been right—Geller had known she wouldn't be able to cope with it. She was merely setting things up for him, just as Hugh had said.

She pulled herself together. What a negative attitude to adopt! She decided to try a different tack. Giving him what she hoped was her 'Gallery manner' smile, she attempted a more conciliatory tone. 'Do you think I could put these down somewhere while we talk for a few minutes? I've been carrying them around for hours.'

Her smile met with a slight narrowing of those disconcertingly blue eyes, but nothing more. After a moment's pause, he cleared one end of what looked like a dining-room table with one sweep of his arm. Books and papers clattered to the floor.

'Here,' he said, and a look of amusement crossed his face at her involuntary expression of disapproval. 'A few more bits and pieces won't make much difference.'

She looked distastefully at the mess on the floor. 'No. I don't suppose they will.' Then she remembered that she was trying not to antagonise him, and the distaste turned to dismay before she told herself to smile.

'I have a letter here from Mr Geller's secretary, if that's any help,' she offered. Of course it wouldn't be. Concocted by Frieda at the last minute, it could do nothing but prove her a bona fide representative of the Gallery, and that was something he hadn't questioned as yet.

Caspar Reissman took the envelope she held out at arm's length, and inserted a finger to tear it along the top. She noticed dark blue paint under his nails.

'I wasn't expecting anything from Antoniou's,' he said, looking at her coolly. Then he grinned. 'Especially not a yellow-eyed Pre-Raphaelite.' His voice was deep, and even in tone—the sort of voice she might have liked, if it hadn't been his.

He glanced at the letter. She could see a few typed lines, signed with Frieda's childish signature and 'p.p. Joseph Geller'. She watched his lashes flicker, and the long mouth turn down a little as he read.

'Well,' he said slowly, 'perhaps you could explain, Miss Bianca James of the Antoniou Gallery. You've been flown here all the way to Florence just to return the portrait I sent to London only a few weeks ago?'

'Not entirely.' Her mind was on the problem of lunch. It was a bit late, but should she take him out? It might be better if he'd had something to drink before she started to insult him. Not that they were her personal insults, but, however tactfully wrapped up, what she had to say wouldn't please him.

She wondered if it was that adrenalin pumping through her now she'd actually got to the critical moment that was making her feel so dizzy. Or maybe it was because she'd left home hours ago without any breakfast.

'Do you mind if I sit down?'

He glanced round, and then dumped the pillows and duvet from the sofa on to the floor. He sat on top of them himself and gestured her to take the vacated space. She sank down, grateful not to have to concentrate any longer on standing upright. Of course, if he'd had any manners, he'd have asked her to sit long before she was ready to collapse at his feet.

'Don't you have any chairs?' she asked, trying to keep any hint of criticism out of her voice. One uncomfortable-looking stool lurked under the table.

There was something like a malicious sparkle in those angelic eyes, but she could have misinterpreted pure amusement. 'Of course—a few. But Monica took them off to a friend of hers to be re-covered. You—er—met Monica.'

'Oh.' For reasons she didn't examine, she had a fleeting impulse to ask about the nature of his relationship with Monica—mistress?—but she resisted the temptation. It was none of her business. But a question about the way he had dragged her, very literally, into the argument was fair enough. Curiosity overcame her discretion. 'Why did you tell her I was your fiancée?'

His tone of voice was offhand, but he was watching her, blue eyes unnervingly narrowed. 'Oh, that. I didn't think you'd understand Italian. Monica wants to marry me again, and it seemed like a heaven-sent inspiration at the time.'

Some inspiration! she thought. But what did he mean by marry him *again*? Was she his ex-wife?

There was an awkward silence. She was very conscious of him on a level that had nothing to do with her job. She debated once more the pros and cons of asking him to lunch. The cons definitely outweighed the pros. A couple of family holidays in Florence as a schoolgirl hadn't exactly equipped her with a list of restaurants suitable for business lunches ... and then, if she did take him somewhere smart, it mightn't occur to him to change his dreadful clothes.

She couldn't help a swift comparison between this scruffy portrait painter and Hugh. There could scarcely be more of a contrast between Hugh's tailored elegance and this individual who looked as though his garments had been thrown on him. But that could, of course, have been carefully contrived on his part. Assessing him critically out of the corner of her eye, she thought that the macho sex-symbol impression she had first formed of him, although not accurate, hadn't been too wide of the mark in some respects. The casual clothes actually revealed rather than hid the strongly muscled frame underneath. The sleeves of his sweatshirt were pushed unevenly up to the elbows, and his forearms were sinewy and dusted with gold hairs. The column of his throat too was powerfully sculpted, and the sloppy garments again accentuated the muscular contours of the wide shoulders, and thighs. There was nothing of the effete artist about this man.

And there was nothing about him that appealed to her, either. All that obvious masculinity amounted to a threat, as she saw it. She preferred her men tall and dark and elegant like Hugh, with quiet good manners.

She took a deep breath. There was no way she was going to risk taking him to lunch. Somewhere in the back of her mind her mother's voice was saying, 'Don't be so conventional, darling—you'll be old before you're twenty-five.' But even her mother couldn't approve of this Horrible Reissman—as a nickname, that appealed to her. Spelt Horribal—like Hannibal . . .

Help—she must try to concentrate. If she made the situation any worse, she could lose her job.

'I work for Antoniou's——' she began.

'We've established that.'

'Yes, well . . . ' She wished he weren't sitting there on that heap of pillows, eyeing her so speculatively. There was something about his look that suggested he was stripping her to the very bones. Maybe he was planning to follow up that kiss by flinging her across a bed, in true macho style?

'You've come to tell me you've brought back the portrait . . . ' He waited, unhelpfully.

This was it. The crunch. There was no getting out of it now.

She regarded him as steadily as she could, ignoring the speculative eyes, and praying for some of the cool 'Gallery manner' she had been practising since she got up, and which had been so notably undermined from

the moment she stood outside the door of Apartment No.
Seven. She cleared her throat. 'Actually, Mr Reissman,
I'm here to collect a portfolio from a dealer and take it
back to London, and it's really Mr Geller who should be
talking to you about this . . . ' If Hugh was right, then it
couldn't do her any harm to shift responsibility on to 'Old
Joe', as Frieda disrespectfully called him. 'Mr Geller has
had to go to a private sale in Geneva,' she went on, 'just
as a slight difficulty over the portrait cropped up, so he
asked me if I could discuss the matter with you in person,
as I was going to be in Florence anyway, and see how
you felt about it . . . '

There was another pause.

'Yes?'

She could sense his hostility. Oh, why had fate decreed
that she should turn up at such a disastrous moment?
She might have handled this if she hadn't been thrown
off balance—again very literally!—by a domestic crisis
that had nothing to do with her. She was breaking the
ground as tactfully as she could, but if she messed up the
next bit there'd be no more trips to Florence, despite her
fluent Italian and Mr Geller's grudging approval of
it—and probably there'd be no more job.

She gave what she hoped was a professional,
businesslike smile. 'I'm sure you understand, Mr
Reissman, that Mr Geller would be handling this matter
personally if he could.'

'Yes?'

'And the Gallery will of course understand if you're
reluctant to . . . to . . . '

'To what?' There was a steely glint in all that blue that
boded no good at all. But, catching his look directly, she
was surprised to find herself wondering whether all the
histrionics with his Monica that she had witnessed earlier
had had anything to do with real anger at all. What she
was seeing now was a glimpse of something far more
intimidating.

She was tempted to throw herself upon his mercy—to
disclaim all responsibility for what she was about to

say—but Mr Geller must have had some confidence in her, and that would be a very unprofessional attitude. If she hadn't been prepared to do the job properly, she should never have accepted it.

She cleared her throat again, nervously. 'As you know . . . the Gallery commissioned the portrait of Mrs Brandt as a compliment to her. She has always had a very significant interest in Antoniou's—financially, I mean, as well as in other ways . . . ' Oh, dear! Should she have said that?

'Mr Antoniou is very grateful to her, obviously. He personally is very pleased with the portrait, of course, but . . . I . . . I don't suppose she saw it at all while you were painting it?'

'A few preliminary sketches from the early sittings, but no, she didn't. I finished it off here in Florence. So she didn't like it?'

She couldn't read his expression, but it didn't make her feel confident. 'It's not exactly that she didn't like it. It's just that—well, people often have a very different image of themselves from the true one, don't they?'

'Stop beating about the bush, Miss Bianca James, and tell me what she wants changed.' The glint in his eyes now was very unpleasant indeed, but whether it was inspired by the Gallery's predicament, or hers, she wasn't sure.

'She . . . she thinks she looks too old,' she began hesitantly.

'And?'

'She wants the colour of the background altered completely—oh, and . . . the frame isn't big enough.'

Silence.

'Anything she does like?'

If panthers could purr, then that was the way they would do it, she thought desperately. Just before they leapt on you, and ripped you to pieces. Whatever she said now would sound like another insult; she was, of course, asking him to repaint the entire portrait.

'And what do you think?'

'But I haven't seen it—or her!' she protested. 'And, anyway, I don't know anything about painting.'

'Then you're in the wrong job,' he said rudely.

Her eyes fired a tawny yellow, but she reminded herself just in time what was at stake, and bit back a reply.

'So what colour does she want the background?' he asked, after another pause.

'Red. It's something to do with the décor of the room in which it's to hang.'

'The colour of her face,' he commented acidly.

She let that pass too. Taking him on in a verbal sparring match wasn't going to get her anywhere. He was so still, sitting there on the duvet, and then there was the way he was watching her—waiting to pounce? He wasn't fully hostile, but she had a strong impression that he didn't think much of her.

Then he said, his voice almost too quiet, 'That portrait's a bloody good likeness. But as you pointed out before, there's no accounting for the way people see themselves. And while we're on the subject, were there any other little details Mrs Brandt or Mr Antoniou or Mr Geller or *you* would like changed?' The sarcasm was knife-edged, but even though she winced inwardly she couldn't help feeling some sympathy with him. If it was a good portrait, then it was an insult to be asked to change it for the sake of one woman's vanity.

'I assure you, Mr Reissman,' she said a little stiffly, 'my own opinions don't enter into this. I merely represent the Gallery.'

'And if I refuse, what are you going to do?'

She didn't answer him directly. 'It's your right, of course, but Mrs Brandt won't allow the portrait to be hung and that will put the Gallery in a very difficult position, since Mr Antoniou commissioned it in the first place as a compliment to her.'

'And are there financial considerations?'

'You mean the Gallery might not pay you?'

'No,' he said with obvious patience. 'I mean how much does the Gallery depend on Mrs Brandt's "financial interests"?' He was too astute. That, of course, was the whole crux of the matter.

Bianca had no idea how the Gallery had originally been funded, or whether it was as successful as its Greek owner, Konstantinos Antoniou, liked it to appear. But it had become evident, during the discussions over the controversial portrait, that the widow of millionaire American metal-box manufacturer Joshua P. Brandt had some sort of controlling interest in Antoniou's. As such, she was a force to be reckoned with.

'I'm afraid I don't know.' It was no less than the truth. 'Mr Antoniou is naturally anxious not to offend Mrs Brandt, and I'm sure he will appreciate the additional work on the painting.' It was a delicate way of saying that Reissman would be paid extra for the finished portrait, but although Mr Geller had told her to hint at this, he had not instructed her to negotiate a fee.

She got up quickly from the sofa, hiding her relief at the prospect of escape, and determined, now she had at last given the message that was her main reason for being in Florence, to get out before he started to ask her any more awkward questions.

'I apologise for taking up so much of your time, Mr Reissman—I realise it was a most inconvenient moment to call on such a matter . . . ' She couldn't resist letting the merest hint of irony creep into her voice as she said that. Served him right for the way he had behaved when she'd arrived! His fiancée indeed—he wasn't the sort of man she'd be seen dead with!

Her thoughts rebellious, she managed a sweet and insincere smile, and continued smoothly, gaining confidence as she went. 'We would naturally be grateful if you could let us know as soon as possible your decision about the portrait. Also, Mr Geller did wonder if you would want to choose the new frame. He'd like to arrange to have it done here since Mrs Brandt is keen to have more gilding on it, in the Florentine style. Of course, if you're not interested in making any specifications for the re-frame, the Gallery will organise it from London.'

He said nothing. So she went on. 'I shall be staying in
Florence most of this weekend—I'm flying back from
Milan on Sunday night—and you can contact me if you
need to. But it would probably be more effective if you
were to call Mr Geller when he returns to the Gallery at
the end of next week.'

Only one thing remained—to give him back the
troublesome portrait. Bianca picked up the larger of the
two packages, hoping that Frieda had been right about
which was which. She saw Horrible Reissman watching
her, sitting lotus-position on his heap of bedding. She
suspected that he had guessed she wasn't sure which
picture to give, and was enjoying it.

Standing over him as she held out the wrapped
package, she was no longer so aware of him as a threat.
She was tall and slim, especially in her high-heeled boots,
and the smart, well-cut lines of her suit were designed to
make her appear slimmer and taller still. She hoped that
this time she could disconcert *him* just a little. It would
be, after all, only a very small consolation for all his
rudeness to her.

Again she put on her 'Gallery smile' as her mother
called it, and adopted her coolest tones. 'Don't get up, Mr
Reissman. I can see myself out.' To her consternation, he
was on his feet in one smooth movement.

'No trouble, Miss Bianca James——' she wished he'd
stop calling her that '—but don't you think we'd better
check you're giving me the right painting?'

He took a knife from a drawer and slit neatly through
the packaging; then, grasping the picture by the stretcher,
he pulled it out.

It was a study of a girl by a table set with plates and
bowls of fruit. The Matisse.

'Oh!' she said, forgetting to hang on to the 'Gallery
manner'. 'I'm most terribly sorry! That's the one I'm
supposed to be taking to the dealer's . . . I think.' Her
confidence evaporated.

Reissman was looking at the painting thoughtfully. He
put it down flat on the table, and turned to her.

'And mine?'

She handed the second picture to him. 'You'd better check this now,' she said apologetically. 'The Gallery was a bit disorganised before I left. We were two members of staff short, and Mr Geller's secretary had rather a lot to do. I'm beginning to wonder what she actually sent to Milan for me to collect!' Visions of an ignominious return swam before her eyes. Instant dismissal!

She watched him anxiously as he slit open the second package. Again he caught hold of the frame, and slid out the picture. This time there was no mistake. He propped it up against the wall, standing it on the table, and they both gazed at it—Bianca in reluctant admiration.

Caspar Reissman was one of the most successful young portrait painters of his generation. Following in his father's footsteps, he had had an ideal start in the art world and could now afford to charge whatever he liked, within reason, for sittings, and was gaining a reputation for being selective about his clients.

The portrait of Mrs Brandt, widow of Joshua P. Brandt, manufacturer and collector, was superb by any standards. He had caught the character so cleverly, the figure on the canvas was almost alive—a lady of formidable egocentricity.

Bianca, awed into complete unselfconsciousness, exclaimed reverently, 'Gosh—what a terrifying woman!'

She was also no beauty, but any change in the portrait would have ruined it. Bianca doubted whether Caspar Reissman would be able to bring himself to add another brush stroke to it. Understanding of his integrity as an artist vied with duty—it was her job to persuade him, she told herself hopelessly. But what on earth could she say?

She found him studying her, not the portrait. He was looking at her intently, with no trace of the humour that had appeared in his face at her ingenuous remark. She had been right about her first impressions of that hard jawline and grim mouth.

'Now I've seen the famous Mrs Brandt,' she began a little hesitantly, 'I know it's a lot to ask, but if you could just ... compromise a bit over the portrait ... ' She trailed off. Obviously now he had had another look at it he had made up his mind he wasn't going to touch it.

'I'll think about it,' he said coldly. Then he looked at the second picture, the Matisse, and back at her. 'Where did this canvas come from?' he demanded.

Taken aback by his tone, she looked at him, her yellow-brown eyes wide. 'I ... beg your pardon?'

'You heard,' he said rudely.

She stared at it. 'It's from the Gallery. I have to deliver it to a dealer at four o'clock.'

He was silent for a few moments. 'How long have you been working for Antoniou's, Miss James?'

'A few months—why?'

'And how did you get the job?'

'Through a friend of a friend—but I really don't see that's——' she was going to say 'any of your business', but decided she couldn't now afford to antagonise him further '—very relevant,' she finished lamely.

'But I think it is, Miss James,' he said, so slowly that she had a terrible sinking feeling about what was going to follow. How could she ever have imagined his eyes were angelic? They'd turned positively arctic! 'I'd like very much to find out exactly what you know about this picture. Because you're going to have to explain to me, before you leave this flat, just how you come to be dealing in forgeries!'

CHAPTER TWO

'WHAT?'

Bianca stared at him in absolute disbelief. The man really *must* be mad—or, for his own reasons, playing some sort of cat and mouse game with her.

It had all sounded so glamorous: jet-setting to Florence for a weekend to deliver a couple of paintings for the Gallery; time to herself, to spend wandering past the little treasure shops of the Ponte Vecchio, and sipping Cinzano in some shady piazza; visiting one of the big museums or idling away an afternoon in the cypress walks of the Boboli gardens . . . It had all seemed so restful and civilised—an exotic version of the life she would like to lead in London, only she wouldn't have Hugh to share it with.

And what had happened? She'd hardly been in the city a couple of hours before she'd been whirled into a total stranger's domestic crisis, and found herself on the verge of being flung into some Italian gaol.

'I don't know what you're talking about!' she protested. 'The only reason I'm here is to deliver a picture and pass on a message on the Gallery's behalf. I assume that *was* the portrait you painted?' Two pink spots had appeared in her cheeks, and her eyes were bright with defensive anger.

'I'm not talking about the portrait—as you very well know.' The voice she had thought she might have liked was now unpleasantly hard, and his eyes were boring into her. 'Sit down, Miss James. It's time you and I got to know each other a bit better. There are some things about you that don't quite add up.'

Caspar Reissman was standing too close for her liking. But it was something more than the intimidation spelled

26

out by his whole attitude that made her retreat almost
involuntarily. Then she found the backs of her legs in
sudden contact with the sofa, and was forced to an abrupt
halt.

'And when we've had our little chat,' he went on, 'I'll
make a few phone-calls. It could be a long afternoon.'

Bianca swallowed nervously. She wouldn't admit to
herself that she might be frightened. Pushed to the back
of her mind, a very disturbing thought was niggling away:
after just one glance he couldn't possibly know the
Matisse was a forgery. It wasn't a well-known work, and
not even an expert could have detected it as quickly as
that. And he had been behaving strangely ever since she
had arrived . . .

No one knew where she was! She should have tried to
phone the Gallery before she set out, to tell them her
destination. She hadn't even mentioned it to the
receptionist at the hotel, and anything might happen to
her in a foreign city—here she was, alone with a stranger
in an obscure apartment, the door was shut, and he had
a knife in his hand!

Somewhere under her ribs a feeling suspiciously like
panic was welling up so fast it was going to choke her
unless she screamed—but she mustn't given in to it,
she told herself. She was Bianca James. She was
twenty-three and worked for a perfectly respectable
gallery in the West End. They had trusted her to do a
routine job for them, and she should have all the
confidence that intelligence, smart clothes and
reasonable good looks could give her.

She mustn't let this extraordinary man see she was
frightened. As she faced him, hoping she looked defiant
even if she didn't feel it, irrelevant details caught her eye,
like the way that the right sleeve of his sweatshirt was
striped with paint—ochre, vermilion, cobalt blue—as
though he had been using it as a rag on which to wipe
his brushes. He must be left-handed.

'Aaah!'

He had caught her off guard, grasping her by one wrist

and twisting her off balance so that she fell back on to
the sofa behind her. Her awkward descent knocked a pile
of papers to the floor. She stared up at him, her feelings,
although she didn't know it, all too clearly visible in her
eyes.

Then the forbidding look vanished. He was suddenly
grinning at her. 'What did you imagine I was going to do
to you, Miss James?' he asked pleasantly.

She opened her mouth, and searched a little
breathlessly for something to say. 'Was that *necessary*?' It
was all the sarcasm she could manage.

'I thought so.' He was quite blatantly enjoying her
discomfiture, the blue eyes sparkling maliciously, but to
her relief he put down the knife, and half sat on the edge
of the table. At least there was now a distance of a few
feet between them.

He swung one leg casually, and folded his arms. She
noticed that the fine gold hair grew thickly on his
forearms and even dusted the back of his hands. His
fingers were spatulate—artist's hands. She swallowed
uncomfortably, her attention caught again by what he
was saying.

'I have far too many nubile girls throwing themselves
at me in all sorts of stages of undress to be interested in
rape . . . ' He was making no effort to hide his amusement.

Her momentary relief turned to annoyance. What had
she been supposed to think when he had grabbed her
like that? Conceited idiot! It didn't help that he had been
able to read her so accurately.

'And although I don't much like you, Miss James,
murder does seem a trifle excessive. Now. What do you
know about this Matisse?' The tone of his voice still
sounded good-natured, but the blue eyes had changed
again.

Bianca had had enough. She would *not* be intimidated
by this—this eccentric lout of an artist, no matter how
important he thought he was! Only minutes ago, she
couldn't have imagined doing anything deliberately that
would have jeopardised her position at the Gallery, and

now quite suddenly she didn't care—if she lost her job, too bad! She would get another one. Geller had been unreasonable all along to expect her to deal with this lunatic.

'I know nothing,' she said defiantly. 'I'm merely delivering it for the Gallery. It's not even the main reason I'm in Florence. I told you—I came to see you about your portrait, and to collect a portfolio to take back to London.'

'And do Antoniou's usually arrange carriage under the arm of an assistant for valuable paintings?' His tone was now quite neutral.

'I've taken care of it,' she said defensively. 'I've only brought it from Milan, anyway—I collected it from customs at the airport. One short train journey . . . '

He was studying her again, critically assessing the details of her face and clothes. She met his eyes fully. She had nothing to hide and wasn't going to let him think she had. 'So you didn't know anything about the painting you were delivering to this dealer? You'd never seen it before?' he went on.

'The Matisse? No, of course not. It was wrapped by Frieda—our secretary—before she sent it on. And, anyway, if I'd known it was a forgery, which I don't believe it is, don't you think I'd have been more careful not to let you see it? But I can't imagine how you think you can identify a fake after one quick glance at it, when it takes experts months of tests to tell a clever copy from the real thing!' She was sounding more successfully scathing now. There was probably no way she could redeem the situation about Mrs Brandt's portrait—Reissman would agree to nothing after this. But then if Hugh was right she hadn't a hope in hell anyway.

She glanced at her watch. She'd allowed herself a reasonable amount of time to interview Reissman, but she didn't want to miss her appointment with the dealer, Pizzi. At least she could get that bit of the assignment right, unless Frieda really had confused the pictures. There'd been a stack of them on the floor of the Gallery, all destined for different buyers, and Frieda did have a cavalier manner with them when Mr Geller wasn't there.

'So you've been working for the Gallery for a few months,' the Horrible Reissman was saying. 'And you got the job through a friend of a friend?'

He really did have the most disconcerting way of looking at her. It almost made her skin prickle.

'Yes, but——'

'This friend of a friend—how well did they know Mr Antoniou or Mr Geller?'

'Why don't you shine a light in my eyes and do the thing properly?' she challenged without thinking, and then regretted her reaction. She suppressed a sigh of exasperation. 'I really don't know the answer to your question, Mr Reissman, and I can't see where all this amateur Gestapo stuff is leading. You can't possibly be right about the Matisse. No doubt you've got some very interesting reasons for your theories, but I've another appointment in an hour and Signor Pizzi is going to wonder what's happened to me. I'm sure you're getting a lot of amusement out of it, but——'

'I don't find it amusing at all, Miss James,' he cut across her. 'I find it very serious. True—you do have to be an expert to tell a forgery in normal circumstances. I admit, I'm not one-hundred-per-cent certain.'

'So how do you know?' she accused.

'I saw it being painted.'

For a moment she couldn't find her voice. 'That's ... that's ridiculous!' she faltered at last. 'And even to me this looks pretty convincing.'

'From that remark I gather you're no expert,' he said coolly. 'This was in fact painted by a friend of mine.'

'How do you know?' she repeated. 'Wasn't he very good at it?'

The sarcasm in the rather childish attempt to score off him wasn't missed by the insufferable Mr Reissman. His voice had an even colder edge to it when he said, 'On the contrary. He's so good at it that he deliberately paints in "mistakes"—or tiny alterations in line or tone—so that his copies can't be sold as originals. I had a very good look at the original when he was painting this—the differences are minute, but they're still there.'

'But surely chemical tests would show the artist was using modern paint and canvas?'

'So what? Johannes isn't a forger. There's an excellent market in good copies these days, and his works are quite sought after in their own right. But they wouldn't fool an expert, and they're not intended to.'

'Supposing this is just being sold as a genuine copy?'

He gave her another of those carefully assessing looks, this time from half-hooded eyes, the keen blue partly veiled by the long gold lashes. 'I think not.'

'How can you be so sure?'

'Assuming this is Johannes' painting—and without Johannes himself seeing it, or some chemical test, obviously I can't be sure—then it should have his signature in the bottom left-hand corner. The original was in a private collection. The owner was thinking of selling it for financial reasons, and he wanted to keep a copy. The copy was signed "Johannes Muller fecit". It's a kind of joke.'

'I know,' she said. 'It's a pun on the Latin, except that "fake-it" is still only a guess, despite everything you've said.'

He met her hostile glare in silence for a few moments, then he said, 'True, but it's a very well-educated guess. To my eyes this has certainly been tampered with by someone who wanted to make it look like the real thing. They spotted the obvious difficulty—the new signature—but they missed Johannes' alterations. And that's why, Miss James, I'd like to know a little more about your involvement with a gallery that handles forged works of art.'

'But Antoniou's is perfectly reputable!' she protested, stung by the automatic assumption that it must be the Gallery—and by implication herself—at fault. 'It's been handling twentieth-century work for years. Mr Antoniou doesn't need to involve himself in petty criminal acts to make his money—he's doing very well.'

'Then why is he so worried about Mrs Brandt?' That hadn't occurred to her, but he didn't give her the chance to reply. 'There are a lot of people who—once they got their hands on something like this—would take care it never crossed the path of an expert. And there are a lot of people who'd happily take an apparently reputable gallery's word on its authenticity. Sold privately, with convincing authentication, this could fetch almost as much money as the original would in the sale-rooms.'

That shrewd blue glance was causing new prickles under her skin, and she was uneasily aware of every movement he made.

'Now what I ask myself, Miss Bianca James, is ... how many people at Antoniou's know already that this is a fake? And does your Mr Pizzi know what he's receiving? Maybe you're all in league, and you've been getting away with this sort of thing for some time. I don't know.'

'But why include me?' she demanded indignantly. 'I told you I don't know anything about this.'

'So you say. But I've only got your word for it. And I've already discovered quite a lot of false impressions about you ...'

There was an odd moment's silence, while that unnerving gaze weighed her up, and she considered his words. What did he mean—false impressions? He might be right about the other employees of the Gallery—very unlikely!—but she knew one thing—he had got her summed up totally wrong. And surely Frieda could never be capable of something like that!

'That's absolute nonsense!' she protested vehemently. 'You've got no reason to say it!'

'Oh, I think I have,' he replied, reverting to the casual tone that was somehow even more insulting. 'Look at the way you're dressed, for example—all geared up to give a completely false image of yourself. It's true I could be a bit biased in my view—you're not my type, and that Romantic style with a capital R is one I particularly detest. Too coyly come-hitherish, and all sublimated sex ...'

Bianca was too astonished—and outraged—to find a

reply. He was the rudest man she had ever met in her life! Artists were supposed to be unconventional, but Caspar Reissman went way beyond that . . . The silence between them was explosive.

Then he said, 'Shall I tell you what your clothes say about the way you want to appear? Yes? No?'

His tone was dispassionate—almost good-natured in fact—consciously attempting to defuse the atmosphere between them, but when she thought about it, he couldn't have been more insulting. And somehow the suggestion that it was purely intellectual judgement, that he took no account of her feelings and didn't find her in the least attractive, made it all the worse. She shouldn't care about it when she didn't like him anyway—but she *did*, although she wasn't going to ask herself why.

She got to her feet, her eyes suddenly blazing. She wasn't sure until she spoke what she was going to say to this hateful man. She took a deep breath.

'I came here, Mr Reissman,' she began unevenly, 'because the Gallery sent me on perfectly legitimate business. I'm sorry if you didn't like what I had to say about your portrait—that had nothing to do with my views. I was merely doing my job. But from the very first moment you've been insulting!'

Warming to her theme, she was even more annoyed that he remained apparently unmoved, smiling in a supercilious way that made her want to hit him. 'How *dare* you speak to me the way you have just now? There is nothing about me that should concern you, except what I have to say on behalf of the Gallery—and I don't happen to like *your* appearance either, if it comes to that! You sum up just about everything I dislike in a man, but at least I've tried not to let my personal disapproval of you interfere with my business here——' She had to pick her way carefully over the mess on the floor as she approached him—sprawling over the heaps of rubbish at his feet would be that last straw! She held out her hand for the painting.

'I'll take the Matisse *now*, Mr Reissman, please,

otherwise I'll be late for my appointment.'

Blue eyes met furious amber-yellow, and held them. Then she found that she was breathing too fast, and, as the impulse of her anger faltered fractionally, she was just a little unnerved. This couldn't be her, caught up in a situation like this! It wasn't real ...

'But I don't think I can let you go, Miss James. Not quite yet,' he was saying quietly. 'I have to make a few enquiries.' His eyes still on hers, he reached out behind him to where her bag lay on its side on the table, and snapped it open. Then, before she had realised his intention, he had extracted the passport she had slipped into the top. She moved quickly to snatch it back, but he whipped it out of her reach.

'Insurance,' he announced calmly. 'There's not much point in your leaving here while I've got this.'

'Give it back! You've no right!' She was really furious now. She grabbed for the passport, and caught his arm, but he was too quick, capturing her wrist with his free hand, and holding the passport out of reach with the other. His grip on her sent an extraordinary feeling through her entire body, yet she couldn't complain that he was hurting her.

'Give it back!' She tried to twist out of his grasp, and would have bitten him if she could. What if it occurred to him to carry on that outrageous kiss where he'd left off? She wouldn't put it past him!

'Calm down.' He didn't sound in the least moved by her angry demand. 'You'll get it back in a while, I promise—Bianca!' She'd tried to kick him through the legs of the table. Then she found herself sitting rather unexpectedly on the floor, her eyes smarting with the suddenness of it. And, to her fury, she discovered he was laughing at her.

'See what I mean about the deceptive Pre-Raphaelite image?' he chuckled. 'A real vixen in disguise!'

He opened her passport and studied it. 'Bianca Catherine James. So you're a student?' He didn't offer to help her up. She decided to stay where she was.

'I was when I applied for that!' she retorted angrily. 'You've no right to take it.'

'Twenty-three years old?'

She didn't answer.

'Height 1.67 metres. Distinguishing marks: none.' He looked at her consideringly. 'Oh, I don't know. I'd say yellow eyes were pretty distinguishing.'

'They're not yellow!' she snapped.

'What would you describe them as?'

'Brown!'

He shrugged. 'Doesn't say much for your colour sense. A bit disastrous for someone who works in the art world, I'd imagine.'

There was another loaded silence.

'So you were born in Siena, Italy. Place of residence: England. British passport. And your name's Bianca. Italian mother?'

'That's none of your business.'

'No. It isn't. But I'm interested.'

She got up from the floor with as much dignity as she could muster, and brushed down her skirt. She thought quickly. Ranting at him did no good—he just changed his tack. Perhaps she'd better change hers. Time was running out. Much as she would have liked to slap that smirk off his face, she'd better be reasonable.

'Look, Mr Reissman, we started off badly when I walked in on your private row—although you did leave the door open——' She tried not to let the way he was looking at her put her off, though she was disturbingly conscious of the nearness of that powerful male body. 'All your theories about the Matisse are very interesting, but they are still just that as far as I'm concerned—theories—and I don't know how you can imagine that I'll believe them. You haven't proved anything, nor can you. So, as I really do have an appointment an hour from now with the dealer who's actually paid for this, I'm afraid I must go.' She was gaining more confidence as she went along. 'Now, if you have any Sellotape, or masking tape, or even string, I'd be really grateful if I could have some to tie up the picture again. And I'd like my passport back, since you've read it cover to cover.'

There was a brief silence.

'Well!' he said at last, with every appearance of admiration. 'That was very good, Miss Bianca James. You've got me even more puzzled than before. Which was it? An act to cover guilty knowledge, or a genuine attempt to deal calmly with an obvious lunatic . . .?'

She could feel the blush creeping up her neck, and she knew it gave her away. He was well aware what she thought of him.

He began to laugh, and ran his hands through the untidy tow-coloured thatch. 'I can't believe this!' he crowed. 'It's the best thing that's happened since Monica stole my credit card!'

His reaction threw her once again—she never knew where she was with him. One moment he was a threat, and the next a paragon of good humour. His shouts of laughter now were completely genuine. She watched him, nonplussed, until he drew a paint-smeared sleeve across his eyes.

'Whew! What a day. Now let's get back to business.' He looked at her, his eyes still sparkling. 'I can't let you go anywhere yet, so why not sit down again and make yourself comfortable? I'm going to make a couple of phone-calls, and, until I've found answers to my questions about that picture, I'm going to have to keep you and the painting under the same roof. Want a glass of wine?'

'No, thank you,' she said primly.

'Suit yourself.' He stuffed her passport into a pocket that started somewhere about thigh level—trust him to have a pocket in a place different from everybody else—and she watched him vanish through an open archway, into what she assumed must be a kitchen.

Without assaulting him, she wasn't going to get the passport back; and even if she could bring herself to resort to violence, she stood no chance of success. Although she was tall, she was slender with comparatively little physical strength, whereas he was alarmingly athletic, and very strong. Anyway, she didn't like the idea of further physical contact with him.

He emerged with an open bottle of red wine, and a glass, and picked his way across to the sofa, prodding the telephone out from underneath it with one foot. Then he sprawled back with the phone on his knee, and winked at her, which she affected to ignore.

'Sit down,' he told her again. 'This could be a long process.' For a moment she was tempted to walk out—why not? He couldn't keep her there unless by force, though he was gambling on the chance that she wouldn't leave without her passport . . . But then there was the question of her responsibility for the painting.

Perched at the table, she watched him as he dialled number after number with no success. The minute-hand on her watch crept round. If he didn't let her go soon, she would have to ring Pizzi to arrange another time to deliver the Matisse.

When finally she stalked over to him, demanding to contact the dealer, he didn't even discuss it. It had crossed her mind, fleetingly, to try to explain her position to Pizzi, but Reissman spoke fluent Italian and would understand every word. And, if he were right about the fake, it might only make things worse.

She got through to a secretary, and told a half-truth about having to delay her first appointment, and said she would ring again. Then she dumped the phone down in the Horrible Reissman's lap, tossed her hair back, adjusted her combs, and returned to her uncomfortable stool.

After what seemed a very long time, he had a conversation in German with someone. She could guess enough to come to the conclusion that whoever it was he was asking for wasn't there. He left some sort of message.

He spoke fast and fluently. Looking again at his colouring, the fair hair and blue eyes, she guessed he must have German blood, even though she had always heard him spoken of as an Englishman. He glanced up once

or twice, to catch her studying him. She flushed, and
hastily looked away, embarrassed at being caught out.
His expression didn't change, and she could tell nothing
of his reactions.

After a while, she glanced at her watch again. Ten past
five. He was still ringing numbers. She was feeling very
tired. It had been a mad rush to get to the airport that
morning, scarcely leaving her time to find the long-term
parking area before a last-minute check-in.

Only a few weeks ago Hugh would have driven her,
but, after that last row over the dinner party she'd
forgotten they were giving she hadn't liked to ask him.
The Customs formalities at Milan had taken ages, though
they had finally accepted her documentation and
relinquished the wrapped, stamped parcels to her. And
the train journey from Milan had taken longer then she'd
remembered. When she finally checked into her hotel
there hadn't been time for anything but a quick wash and
brush-up before she started out again—for her
appointment with Caspar Reissman.

To think she'd actually been looking forward to
meeting the well-known painter! It would have been
impressive to have been able to say casually, 'Caspar? Oh,
yes, I've met him,'—omitting, of course, all reference to
the fact that it was only for a few minutes, on an errand
for the Gallery. And how wrong could you be? He was
in no way what she had expected.

If he didn't make some progress soon, she'd be there
all night.

She studied him again under her eyelashes. He was
now talking Italian very fast, and gesturing as he spoke.
He seemed to be able to switch languages with the ease
most people changed their clothes. She found herself
watching those large, well-shaped artist's hands until,
catching his eye again, she looked away in confusion.

The trouble was he fascinated her, and she found her
gaze being drawn towards him almost against her will.
So for a while she stared deliberately at the polished
table-top—as much of it as was visible under the

clutter—and thought about that. At least it was polished, so somebody must clean the flat sometimes. Perhaps it was Monica. Was she his ex-wife, perhaps? He had said something about her wanting to marry him again—and about her having the chairs re-covered. That sounded very wifely. Or she could just be his mistress . . . And what was all that bedding doing strewn over the sitting-room? Perhaps they'd had a row the night before, and she'd refused to sleep with him. It was difficult to imagine anyone wanting to sleep with that lunatic—although she had to admit there was something about him, if you liked that sort of downbeat image, all casual strength and untidiness. But Monica couldn't be more wrong if she saw her as a rival—his fault, of course. Anyway, none of it was her business.

Idly, she traced invisible patterns with her finger. Once he'd made his silly phone-calls, would he let her go? She wanted to get back to her room in the hotel, have a shower and change, and then have a quiet dinner somewhere and go to bed . . . Would he never finish?

She wondered if she should try to ring Hugh later, when she got to the hotel. Only a couple of months ago she'd have been counting the minutes until she could expect to find him in his flat, but now—well . . . things had got so complicated between them.

It wasn't only because of that stupid dinner party. Luckily she had realised, in time for Hugh to hire a cook, that he had been expecting her to organise things the very night on which she had long been committed to attending the private view. Both of them had firmly believed that they had told the other about their arrangements for that evening, and it was impossible to sort out who was wrong and who was right. Hugh, however, had been more annoyed underneath than she had—he hated carefully organised plans to go wrong. But she suspected that there was more to it than just the party.

From the first her relationship with Hugh had been so much more than anything she had experienced before. He was her ideal, the man who matched up to all her earlier adolescent dreams. Tall, slim, dark and good-looking, he worked in a merchant bank, and was already tipped for success. The City sophisticate one of her friends called him, and she desperately wanted to match that image herself.

The general opinion among their friends was that they complemented each other beautifully: both tall, with striking good looks, Hugh having the cool financial brain and cool manner to match, and Bianca the lively artistic flair, which showed in her individual clothes and in her influence on the house she shared with friends in Fulham. But she wasn't so sure now.

By nature she was passionate and impulsive, and she'd had to learn to suppress many of her spontaneous reactions in Hugh's company; because she admired him so much she had told herself it was a good thing. She wore what he approved of, and said what he approved of, and spent nearly all her free time with him.

When their romance had turned into an affair, Hugh had been very keen that she move in with him in his flat just off Sloane Square. Large, quiet and elegant, it was better in every way than the house she shared in Fulham. But something had kept her from giving up her own base, although it had turned into a subject for disagreement between them. She hadn't had that sort of independence long, and she had been loath to relinquish it so soon. Time enough when Hugh mentioned marriage.

She had never intended to have an affair with someone she wasn't going to marry. And she had been certain that, one day, she was going to marry Hugh. Just now things were difficult between them, but her belief in their future hadn't really changed.

'No, I can't tell you that,' Caspar Reissman was saying in Italian. 'I have to speak to Johannes first.'

What would be Hugh's reaction if she told him she'd been virtually kidnapped by a mad painter who thought she was involved in some forgery racket? And that he'd actually kissed her within minutes of meeting her? No, it wouldn't be a good idea to tell him that, and anyway she wasn't too keen to think about that kiss . . . She pictured him, standing by the antique sideboard he'd picked up at an auction, his dark head bent over the phone. He'd probably give that dismissive smile of his—assuming, of course, that he'd forgiven her for last week—and then ask her something about her train journey.

If she wanted a more dramatic response, it'd be much more fun ringing her mother. She imagined the horrified squawk on the other end of the line. 'Darling! How frightful! Why didn't you hit him over the head with a bottle of turps?' Her mother had one of those husky voices that split into two registers in moments of excitement. It was supposed to be very sexy. A pity you couldn't inherit something like that. Bianca's own voice was far too sweet and clear to be anything but . . . well, Victorian. But Hugh had once said he liked it.

She looked at her watch again. Six o'clock—and she'd thought this interview would take no more than half an hour! When she glanced up again, she found Caspar Reissman watching her. He had put the telephone down on the sofa next to him, and was sitting back at his ease, hands behind his head, one ankle crossed over his knee. It was easy to see why his trousers were shapeless and baggy if he sat around like that most of the time.

'Well?' she demanded. 'Have you at last satisfied yourself that I'm not at the centre of some international forgery ring?'

'No. I haven't.'

'You mean to say that after keeping me here unnecessarily for over five hours, making me change my appointment with a dealer, you haven't achieved anything?' The sheer effrontery of it almost took her breath away—who *did* he think he was? Then she remembered her mother's warning: count fifty. There wasn't time for that, but she wouldn't achieve anything by getting worked up.

'Mr Reissman, judging by your life-style, you seem to operate according to different rules from everyone else, but I assure you that in the real world—which I come from—what you're doing is quite unacceptable! You have no right to take my passport and try to keep me here. If there is a question of forgery, which I don't believe for a minute, then it's for the police to deal with, not you.'

He didn't answer immediately, but the grin had faded.

'I quite agree with you,' he said, unexpectedly. 'But look at it from my point of view. A girl—sorry, young woman—turns up here with a picture. I only see it by accident. I'm convinced it's a copy done by a friend of mine, and I have reason to suspect it's being passed off as the genuine article. This woman says she knows nothing about it. It sounds like the truth, but is it wise to believe her?' He was using his hands again as he spoke, to reinforce and illustrate in a way that was wholly un-English—the way her mother did. 'The woman walks out of my flat with the painting, and I never see it or her again. I'm still convinced it's a fake, but where's my evidence? Your eyes have gone completely yellow—you must be furious. Did you know that happened when you're angry?'

'I am angry!' she blazed at him. 'You've already made your mind up about me, about the painting, the Gallery—everything!'

'No, I haven't,' he said calmly. 'I thought I'd made that clear. But for the moment, I can't let you go. Not without some hold on you—hence the passport.'

She thought furiously, chewing her lip, and then hating the idea, she offered, 'Suppose I come back tomorrow.'

'And leave the painting here?'

'Yes—no!' How could she possibly leave it? It was worth a great deal of money, and she was responsible for it. Supposing he took it away somewhere and it never reached Pizzi? How could she ever explain it to Mr Geller?

'Then no deal,' he said firmly.

If she wouldn't leave without her passport, and couldn't leave without the painting, and he refused to give in on either of them, then they had obviously reached stalemate.

Across a few feet of untidy floor they assessed each other—Bianca openly angry, and Caspar Reissman apparently relaxed and inscrutable. But for all his superficial ease, she was conscious of some tension or hostility in him that was reacting on her. Again, without doing anything, he seemed to pose a kind of threat—she didn't know whether it was his size, or that casually powerful physique, or just the fact that he had made it clear that he disapproved of so much about her, but he made her feel nervous. She was acutely aware of herself and him. And she couldn't forget that he had kissed her.

'Do you belong to the strict Temperance Society, Miss James, or are you merely a member of Alcoholics Anonymous?'

'What?' Caught up in the turmoil of her own reactions to him, she wasn't prepared for the change of direction.

'You don't drink?'

'Yes, I do, but——'

'Good. Then I suggest you have some wine. There are glasses in the kitchen. Johannes will be ringing me after nine o'clock—which could mean nearer twelve. It's going to be a long night.'

If she had known exactly how long a night it was going to be, she reflected, a considerable while afterwards, she might have followed the path of Monica's possessions earlier that day, and leapt over the balcony herself.

CHAPTER THREE

WHY did she have all her clothes on? She felt cramped and the light was strange. She must be late for work—no, it was Saturday. Yesterday . . . Florence . . . Caspar Reissman's flat! She sat bolt upright. The room was every bit as untidy as it had been the night before. She looked at her watch. Half-past nine!

The flat was silent. Did that mean her kidnapper—it was the only way to think of him—was in bed, or did it mean he had gone out to fetch the *carabinieri*? She listened intently for a while. He must. be out—there wasn't a sound.

She reviewed the situation. She was very hungry, and she was very tired—which wasn't surprising. She hadn't been able to lie down to sleep until long past midnight, and that was only after another row with Caspar about going back to her hotel.

'There's no way you're leaving this flat,' he had argued, when the expected phone-call from Germany had finally come through. 'Everything I've heard from Johannes only confirms my suspicions. I need time to get proof, and Johannes has to make some contacts. I can't let you go.'

'But I'm not a criminal!' she protested furiously. 'No matter how long your wretched Johannes spends interrogating people, that's something he'll never be able to prove—and I'm not staying here! I want to spend the night in my hotel!'

'I never said you were a criminal, but I can't let you go. You can sleep here just as well,' he'd added callously. 'There's a lot of Monica's stuff lying about. Use that. She won't mind.'

'I'm not sleeping in here!'

She didn't like to remember the unpleasant grin he'd

given her. 'Where else do you suggest—in my bed with me?'

Nor did she like to remember the way his eyes had assessed her as she struggled for a suitably scathing reply—but he was there before her. 'I've already told you, you're not my type. So you needn't stay awake all night wondering when I'm going to rape you.'

And that was how she had come to be lying, almost fully dressed, on the sofa. She'd used the pillow she'd found on the floor only when she'd got an impossible crick in her neck from the arm of the sofa, and the duvet when she'd grown so cold she couldn't do anything but lie there and shiver.

Her jacket was hanging on the back of a chair, and she'd taken her boots off. She still wore the rest of her clothes. She didn't really trust him, no matter what he'd said, and staying fully dressed had made the whole arrangement seem less permanent.

She was very worried about her skirt—it would be impossibly crushed, and she hadn't brought anything else as smart with her. If Caspar really was out she might be able to take it off and iron it. Someone like Monica, wife or no wife, would surely keep an iron here, even if *he* pressed his shirts under the mattress, or wore no shirts at all.

The first thing she saw when she crawled painfully off the sofa was a large piece of paper propped up against the half-empty bottle of wine on the table. It occupied the only clear space.

The handwriting was beautiful—clear, flowing italic. 'Good morning, hostage! Have gone out to buy some breakfast. I assume you want some. The door is double-locked, the neighbours are deaf, and even Monica wouldn't jump off the balcony.'

The text was illuminated by a border of vine leaves, on which several unmistakably prissy young women stood; in the top left-hand corner a crude little satyr tempted one of them with a bunch of grapes. Reissman couldn't have been more insulting. She tore it into tiny pieces, and scattered them like confetti on the floor. He'd never even notice the additional mess.

She'd had no food at all for hours. One of those timeless meals had been served on the aircraft, but she had left it all. Then the events of the previous night had made eating irrelevant. A portrait painter, it seemed, rarely thought of food, although he consumed at least a bottle and a half of wine before he went to bed.

She had refused all invitations to drink.

'Why?' he had asked, with a sardonic lift of one fair eyebrow. 'Do you suspect it's a preliminary to my having my evil way with you, in spite of what I said?'

She couldn't make him out. Insulting and critical of her appearance, he still didn't miss an opportunity to pass provocative remarks that she found very unnerving. It would have made more sense to leave her alone.

She had tried to look at him with the contempt he deserved, but it hadn't had much effect on him. He had laughed.

His friend Johannes—'The Forger', as she'd christened him—wasn't it asking for trouble to paint virtually foolproof copies?—hadn't rung until after midnight. Bianca had thought she was going to die of exhaustion. She had ended up curled up on the sofa, her face hidden in her arms, full of despair. Although she couldn't believe that Caspar intended to harm her, he obviously wasn't going to let her go until he had solved the mystery of the Matisse. All she could do was pray he'd find out before it was too late for her to arrange to see Signor Pizzi, hand over the documentation, and collect his receipt acknowledgement as well as the portfolio she was to take back to Antoniou's.

Exploration of the untidy flat revealed an attractive bathroom, surprisingly clean; a large converted studio stocked with canvases, paints and easels; a master bedroom with a large, unmade double bed in the middle of it—mercifully unoccupied—and a kitchen. Now she had established Caspar's absence, she went boldly into the latter and looked round for an iron.

When she finally discovered one, she plugged it into a socket in the sitting-room to heat it up. There was no ironing board. She felt very sorry for Monica. Could she possibly be the painter's wife? No—not if he'd pretended he was engaged to Bianca herself. And, anyway, she couldn't imagine anyone promising to love and cherish a character like Reissman, even if they did find him attractive, though to be fair, he really did have a very powerful kind of appeal—if you liked that sort of thing, of course. Which she didn't.

She took off her skirt quickly, spread out what she guessed must be one of Monica's sheets on the floor, in a space she cleared simply by heaping up the jumble, and laid the skirt on it. Then she started to press it. She would have to get a move on—Caspar might come back at any moment.

She was about half-way through the process when she heard a key in the lock of the front door. The door opened into only a token lobby, really part of the living-room. She was on her hands and knees in her petticoat, which was black, with a lace-edged split up the side—not something she wished to be seen in by Caspar. And she hadn't even combed her hair.

The door opened, and she looked up, not quite sure whether to brazen it out or flee.

She found herself staring at the woman called Monica. The staring was mutual.

Monica's Italian was fast, idiomatic and to the point. 'Why the *hell* are you here?' she demanded.

She had amazingly thick lashes—or she wore a great deal of mascara. Bianca was instantly critical, her reaction conditioned by Hugh who didn't approve of the heavily make-up look.

Monica's eyes narrowed in suspicion. It wasn't difficult to see what was going through her mind. 'Where's Caspar?'

'Gone to get some breakfast,' Bianca replied in Italian, before she realised how the information must sound.

The Italian woman was wearing the fur coat Bianca had last seen airborne, flying heavily over the piazza with one of Monica's shoes. She was fashionably dressed, and she had an expensive scarf and bag. The hostility in her face prompted Bianca to keep a grim hold on the iron.

'He has told me nothing of you—nothing!' Monica began accusingly. 'Then one morning—paff!' She made an eloquent gesture. 'And you are here! Now I tell you'—she was advancing slowly, one hand on hip, to where Bianca still knelt, iron in hand, on the floor—'I'm not giving him up. Caspar and I have known each other like *that*'—she crossed two fingers expressively—'for many years.'

Bianca blinked.

'So don't think that because he likes you in his bed for a little while your marriage will last.' Monica laughed theatrically. 'It won't!'

I don't believe this! Bianca was thinking. She's like some character out of a play! Is this the way she and Caspar go on at each other all the time?

'I think you've made a mistake——' she began.

'I make a mistake? No, it's *you* who are making the mistake, and I'm warning you—I'm not giving up! It would be better for you to decide to finish with him now. You can't mean very much to him if he's still seeing me behind your back—and make no mistake, *cara* . . . ' she put all the sarcasm she could manage into the word ' . . . he won't stay faithful to you while I'm around!'

'But I'm not his fiancée!' Bianca protested. 'I never even saw the man before yesterday!'

'Then why did he tell me you were? He shouted it—for the whole piazza to hear! And then he told me again when he came down to the street. He said he'd met you in England, and you'd come to Florence to get married.' Monica's dark eyes flashed dangerously.

'That's ridiculous! He never even knew of my existence until I turned up on the doorstep. I don't know how to convince you . . . ' Bianca looked round helplessly, and then saw Mrs Brandt's portrait stacked against the table-leg where Caspar had left it. Abandoning the iron, she seized it, and held it up to Monica. 'Look—if you know anything about Cas—Mr Reissman,' she corrected herself quickly, 'you must know he sent this to a gallery in London a few weeks ago. I work for that gallery, and I've returned it to him so that he could make changes to it.'

Monica glanced at it dismissively. 'That proves nothing,' she said contemptuously. 'And it doesn't explain why you're sleeping with him!'

What was the matter with these people? Bianca asked herself despairingly. First she was accused of being criminally involved in a forgery racket, and then of spending the night in the arms of a mad painter she'd never met before in her life—and, even more insulting, he was the last man on earth she'd contemplate having any sort of relationship with, if she could only get out of his flat!

She took a deep breath. Count fifty! I'm half-English, she told herself. I'm not going to behave like an Italian prima donna on a bad night at the opera—come to think of it, that summed up Monica nicely. Could she be a singer or an actress? It would explain quite a lot.

The way to handle this was to regard it as useful practice in dealing with difficult customers at the Gallery. 'Monica,' she said patiently, 'I've got a fiancé in England'—not strictly true, just anticipating events—'and I have a job to do here. If your horrible Mr Reissman would give me back my passport, and the painting I should be taking to a perfectly respectable dealer, I'd be out of here so fast you wouldn't see me for dust!'

'Why has Caspar got your passport?'

Bianca sighed. 'It's a long story, but he thinks I'm a criminal.'

Monica stared at her, suspicious, unwilling to believe her. Then her expression changed. 'My sheet!' she shrieked.

There was an undeniable smell of burning. Bianca snatched up the iron, and Monica whipped the sheet away from under it, but it was not only the sheet that had suffered—there was a clear scorch-mark on the dark cloth of Bianca's skirt.

'Oh, no!' she wailed. 'What on earth am I going to wear?
I can't go out in this!'

The state of Bianca's wardrobe was irrelevant to the
Italian. 'You were sleeping in my bed?' she demanded.

'I certainly wasn't in Mr Reissman's! If you're talking
about the sofa, then yes, I was—but it wasn't through any
choice of mine, I can assure you——'

Monica opened her mouth, but Bianca could guess the
trend of her thoughts, and went on before she could
interrupt. 'And before you accuse me again of being after
your precious Caspar—though I can't imagine what you
see in him—I've been booked into a perfectly respectable
hotel since yesterday, and I've never even got so far as to
unpack my clothes! I'm sorry about your sheet, I really
am. I'll buy you another one. But I don't want that horrible
man coming back and finding me like this . . . '

Helplessly she indicated the black petticoat, with its
provocative lace split up the side.

Monica's mouth opened and shut rather quickly this
time, and she looked at Bianca for a few moments, a
puzzled frown on her face. Then something that had been
said must have finally made an impression. 'OK,' she said
decisively. 'We have to talk.' And she stripped off the
heavy fur in a businesslike way. She sat down, legs crossed
elegantly, on the sofa, and searched her bag for a cigarette.
'You smoke?'

Bianca almost wished she could have said yes, since
the offer was the equivalent of the Red Indian peace pipe,
but she shook her head.

Monica drew in a long breath, and then exhaled slowly.
She laughed, her black eyes sparkling through the blue
haze. 'Caspar won't like this—he hates cigarettes in his
apartment. He used to make me go out on the balcony.'

The use of the past tense struck Bianca as odd, but she
didn't pursue it.

Once she had decided to listen, the Italian quickly
grasped the essentials of Bianca's story. 'We must see how
we can help each other,' she declared finally. 'You want
to be out of here—I want to be in. You saw how he threw

me out yesterday.'

'Monica . . .' she said hesitantly. 'Were you and Caspar married?' Now she had said it, it didn't sound any better than asking what she really suspected—are you and Caspar lovers? She would have to be his ex-wife anyway, since his claim to be engaged to Bianca herself wouldn't have made any sense at all otherwise.

Monica blew out an angry stream of smoke. 'Married!' she exclaimed contemptuously. 'That man doesn't even know the existence of the word! He believes in absolute freedom for the artist—at least, that's what he says.'

'You don't believe it?'

'Oh, yes, I believe it,' she replied grimly. 'We started an affair three years ago, and where am I now? Out in the piazza with the begonias.'

Bianca laughed. She was beginning to like Monica—at least she had a sense of humour.

'What were you fighting about?' she asked, curiosity for a moment side-tracking from the more pressing issues.

'Oh, money. It is always money. And you, with your fiancé—you fight about money?'

Bianca couldn't imagine herself ever having the sort of row with Hugh that she had witnessed between Monica and Caspar Reissman—Hugh was far too controlled. He withdrew into himself when he was angry, and he disliked displays of temper in other people. Often she didn't find out the cause of their more difficult patches until long afterwards. They had disagreements, yes, but never fights. There was, of course, their latest difference of opinion over the dinner party, but you couldn't call that a real row.

'No.' She shook her head. 'We don't actually fight.'

Monica looked at her as though she didn't believe her. 'Then you aren't in love with him,' she pronounced.

Bianca, a little taken aback, smiled. 'Oh, yes, I am!' she assured her. 'It's very romantic—and very civilised.'

The rather critical reflection on her own relationship with Caspar passed unremarked by Monica. 'You are not in love with him,' she reiterated firmly. 'You cannot be, and have a truly Latin temperament.'

'I'm half-English.'

Monica raised artistically plucked eyebrows. 'Really? But you speak Italian perfectly! Much better than Caspar. He is good,' she added grudgingly, 'but not so idiomatic.'

'My mother's Italian, and I've spent virtually every holiday in Italy since I was a child.'

Monica laughed. 'Then, as one Italian to another, I tell you we've got to stick together—and I also tell you you're not in love with your English fiancé. When you're really in love you're like one person, even though you are two, and that is why you fight . . . oh!' She threw up her hands and raised her eyes in mock despair. 'I can't explain properly.'

'The English are different,' Bianca joked. 'Everyone says it's to do with the climate—you can't have passionate rows in a country where it rains all day! Anyway, I happen to admire men who remind me of my English father. He was in the Diplomatic Service, and everyone's idea of a perfect English gentleman.'

Monica shrugged, and then gave her a grin. 'OK,' she said. 'So you're looking for another man like your father, but if he was that perfect you'd do better to look for something quite different—you won't find another one like him. And now—how can we help each other?'

Their initial misunderstandings once sorted out, Bianca found she got on very well with Caspar Reissman's mistress. If she hadn't been naggingly aware all the time that the subject of their conversation might return at any minute and put a stop to the conspiracy, she would have liked to gossip at much greater length.

She discovered that Monica had had her last major row with the painter over another man, with whom she had had a brief affair during one of their cooling-off periods. They had had quite a few of those, it seemed, in the past couple of years, despite Monica's frequent assertions that she was mad about him. Major rows, as opposed to minor ones, involved being flung out.

'So it was a major one I walked in on?' Bianca asked,

fascinated in spite of herself by these unexpected glimpses into Caspar's private life.

Monica pulled a face. 'Oh, not so much this time,' she said in offhand tones. 'He's just more of a *bastardo* these days.'

Finally, it was agreed between them that, the key to Bianca's present predicament being the Matisse, the sooner it was out of Reissman's clutches the better. Once he had lost the so-called 'evidence' for his suspicions, he could have no further interest in keeping Bianca a virtual prisoner. He could therefore hand over her passport, and she could move out, enabling Monica to move speedily back in.

Monica couldn't have cared less whether or not the painting was a fake. She was utterly single-minded in her pursuit of Reissman, and her determination to get Bianca out of the flat.

'It's quite obvious,' she said crossly, 'that he's using you to keep me out of here. Why else tell me that you were his fiancée? Does he think I'm so stupid that I won't find out?'

'I think he underestimates you!' Bianca said with a smile. And then her smile widened, lighting her eyes. 'You know, I was annoyed with Mr Reissman last night when he said he hadn't had so much fun since you stole his credit card—I'd love to know about that some time—but now I'm beginning to think *I* haven't had so much fun for years!' Then her smile faded. 'You *are* sure you'll be all right taking that Matisse to the dealers? I'm not supposed to let it out of my hands for one second, and it'd be too awful for words if anything happened to it—or you, of course,' she added hastily.

'No problem.' Monica got up, reaching for the heap of expensive fur carelessly tossed over the sofa. 'Together we will get the better of that *bastardo*—all men are the same, and it is bad for them to think that they can be too clever.'

She left a couple of minutes later with the painting, hastily rewrapped, under her arm. She had also agreed to go to Bianca's hotel to fetch her some clothes, and bore a scribbled note by way of authorisation. Bianca was to ring the hotel before she arrived to avoid difficulties.

What she'd told Monica was true. She was beginning to enjoy herself very much now that there was a possibility of outwitting Caspar. Once the flamboyant Italian had left, however, Bianca was again racked by doubts about the wisdom of handing over the controversial Matisse. Monica was an undisciplined, theatrical sort of character. Still, she had reason to trust her, if only because she was so set on regaining her foothold in the flat. 'And the best of British luck to her!' Bianca thought with a smile. From what she had seen and heard already, she and Caspar deserved each other.

There was still no sign of her unpredictable kidnapper, and it was impossible to resist the temptation to have a bath. Monica, now that a conspiracy had been established between them, had offered her freely the use of any of her possessions still in the apartment. But there was surprisingly little for someone who claimed to be living there. She managed to find a bath-towel which looked clean, and which Monica had asserted was hers.

She took off all her clothes in the bathroom, and had a hasty shower. If Caspar came back she didn't want to have to emerge half dressed, looking for stray garments. If only she could have got to the hotel!

She heard him open the door with his key just as she turned off the water. She dried herself and dressed quickly—and then realised she'd have to emerge swathed toga-fashion from the waist down. She'd forgotten about the singed skirt, left hanging over the back of the sofa. She'd also forgotten her comb.

She examined herself in the mirror, wiping away the steam impatiently. She'd caught her hair up with a clip to keep it out of the way, but the device hadn't been very successful. Damp tendrils curled round her face and down her back. It wasn't strictly Pre-Raphaelite, but Caspar could be forgiven for calling it Victorian. Her features too contributed to that impression: delicate bones, fine skin, and large eyes—but they definitely didn't belong to those grey-eyed Burne-Jones ladies he so despised. They were a clear, pale golden brown. Certainly not yellow.

Damn. Her make-up was in her bag at the hotel. She felt she needed all her disguise to deal with someone like Reissman; it helped if you could project a slightly chic, sophisticated image. For all he had said about creating false impressions—and that still annoyed her—people did deal with you at face value.

Now it was time to enter Round Two. Round One, grudgingly, she had to concede to Caspar, but with Monica on her side it was a whole new game. Had he discovered that the painting had disappeared yet? Possibly not. There had been no howl of baffled rage.

She had to nerve herself to leave the bathroom.

'So you're alive,' he greeted her as she entered the living-room, assessing her with eyes that took in every detail from the undisciplined curls to the sari-style folds of Monica's bath-towel. 'Earlier this morning you looked dead to the world.'

It embarrassed her to discover that he'd watched her while she was asleep; she was instantly on the defensive, as though he'd taken advantage of her in some way. She felt again those unnerving prickles sliding about under her skin as he pursued his leisurely inspection of her, and despite the fact they were several feet away from each other, it was almost as though he were touching her. She tried not to betray the effect he was having on her. Every inch of her, covered or not, felt naked to that critical gaze.

Just when she thought she could sink into the floor with embarrassment, he said, 'The new look's a definite improvement on yesterday. May we hope for even better things as the day progresses?' The light sarcasm in his tone annoyed her, and quickly brought her back to her senses. She tried to treat him to the same bone-stripping appraisal, but she couldn't manage it with anything like his casual insolence.

He had made a marginal improvement on the day before—at least his denim jeans looked clean and relatively new, and the navy crew-necked sweater he was wearing was recognisable as cashmere. He might even have combed his hair, since it didn't stick up quite so much, but he still hadn't shaved.

'I gather you found my note?'

'Yes, thank you.' The confetti was no longer in evidence. A glance round the sitting-room revealed that he must have been tidying up while she was in the bathroom. Not that there was any real improvement, but some space had been created on the floor by dumping spilled papers and books on to the sofa.

He looked highly amused about something.

'Have some breakfast?'

'No, thank you.'

That long, rat-trap mouth quirked at one corner. 'No, I suppose it would spoil the suffering Lizzie Siddal look.'

'The *what*?' She had only to be in his company for a couple of minutes, and already she was losing the sense of humour that had been restored by Monica. He did have the most unfortunate effect on her.

'Mistress of that idiotic poser Dante Gabriel Rossetti,' he explained helpfully. 'She died of consumption and opium. For someone who professes to work in an art gallery, you don't know much.'

Of course she should have remembered.

'For someone who professes to hate Pre-Raphaelites,' she retaliated, 'you take a flattering amount of interest in them!'

He was still studying her, noting with obvious amusement the blush she could feel in her cheeks. 'They exercise a morbid fascination.' She might have known he'd have an answer. Then he added, in a tone that she interpreted instantly as genuine conceit, 'I know a lot about everything. Art's my business.'

'You're insufferable!' The words were out before she'd realised she'd said them. Her hand flew to her mouth, and she looked at him in alarm, but it had long been too late to remember she was supposed to be tactfully negotiating alterations to the portrait of Mrs Brandt.

Somewhere along the line this impossible individual had stopped being the famous Caspar Reissman whose name she had been so keen to drop, and had become just Caspar . . . an infuriating man who insulted her and provoked her, and maybe even fancied her, for all he'd said initially about her not being his type . . . a case of opposites being attracted? No, that definitely didn't apply from her point of view. Although if she was honest, when she wasn't being irritated by him she was quite entertained by him—and what she'd said to Monica was true: she hadn't had so much fun for years . . .

He didn't seem to have taken offence at her unguarded exclamation. Clearly amused by the gesture, he said, 'Good! I'm keeping it that way. It makes for an independent life.' He ran a hand through the tow-coloured hair, making it stand briefly on end. 'Coffee?' he offered, and, without waiting for a reply, headed for the kitchen.

She was starving, and the prospect of coffee would have been heaven, but, like Persephone in the old Greek myth, she felt that if she accepted one drop of drink from him, or one crumb of food, she'd never get away at all. He still had her passport to the outside world.

Unwillingly, she followed him into the kitchen and watched him getting butter out of the fridge, and measuring coffee into the percolator. Again she noticed the shape of his hands—long bony fingers with those wide spatulate ends. Sensitive, artist's hands . . . Well, all his sensitivity must be reserved for his oils and canvas, because he didn't show too much of it where people were concerned.

'What was Monica doing here?' he asked pleasantly.

'Wh—what?'

He had done it again, taken the wind out of her sails when that was the piece of news she had been saving up to announce to him, at a moment of maximum advantage to herself.

'The lady with the unusual red hair who was here while I was out. You met briefly yesterday.'

'I didn't say *who* . . . ' she stalled ' . . . I said what—I meant, what do you mean?'

'I mean, what was she here for?'

'Why did you tell her I was your fiancée?' The only defence in this case was attack.

He was opening drawers, and had turned on a tap. He didn't raise his voice and she had to go fully into the kitchen not to miss what he was saying.

'Oh, it made the point, I suppose. Throwing Monica out is getting to be my occupational therapy, but I imagine her version was something about my impossible tempers and how she walked out on me yet again?'

'No, she——' Then Bianca stopped. How could she have fallen for that so easily? There was no point in denying it now: she'd more or less admitted to Monica's visit. But she needn't let him know they were in league.

Then he said, 'I know about the painting, by the way.' He banged a drawer shut and turned to face her, folding his arms and leaning back against the sink casually. 'I met Monica in the street a few minutes ago, on her way back from your friend Signor Pizzi. She couldn't wait to tell me how she'd got the better of me. Whose idea was it—yours or hers?'

The suggestion had initially come from Bianca, but she didn't get much satisfaction from the admission.

'Mine,' she said, lifting her chin defiantly. 'And now you've got no reason to keep me here any longer!'

He met her look fully, his own eyes cold. 'That's just where you're wrong. It's true that I can't get the painting back—according to Monica it's now in the hands of one of Pizzi's assistants—but I've just got a telex via a friend's office. It supports my version of the story rather than yours. I'll leave you to ponder all the implications of that, but just in case you've missed the main point, your attempt to make away with the evidence this morning begins to look like complicity. Our friend Monica's a fool—she's incapable of seeing much beyond her own concerns, and she would probably believe anything you told her. You, I'm not so sure about. That wet-behind-the-ears look's a bit too good to be true . . . '

It wasn't said as a joke about the shower. Although annoyed by his manner, she was also chilled by the thought that only a few minutes before she had been certain she had managed to outwit him. Now, with every appearance of pleasantness, he was in the same breath offering her breakfast and telling her that he was ready to hand her over to the police. As for fancying her in any way, that had been a complete delusion on her part. His designs on her began and ended with the fact that he thought she was a crook.

'I'll say one thing for Monica!' she flung at him rather desperately. 'At least she can recognise the truth when she hears it! You wouldn't know it if it came up and hit you—you've been jumping to one wrong conclusion after another ever since I got here!'

'Ah!' he said, his eyes suddenly sparking a dangerous blue. 'It so happens that the proposition on which my arguments rest is about to be proved true—that telex this morning helps to confirm it. And so, my little English miss, you'd better consider your story very carefully, because if there are weak places in it you can be sure I shall find them . . . I don't like to think that my friend is being cheated, and made to look like a criminal by people like you.' The quiet voice held an implicit threat.

'But you haven't once stopped to think how you're making *me* look!' she protested, suddenly very miserably aware that she was tired, hungry, and exceedingly ill-equipped to deal with this man—and if she wasn't careful she was going to humiliate herself by crying with sheer frustration. 'You're convinced I'm guilty because you haven't for a moment considered anything but your own version of the story!' There was a treacherous little catch in her voice. 'OK, so perhaps the painting is a forgery—I only say *perhaps*—but that doesn't have to make me guilty of anything, or Mr Geller, or Frieda, or Mr Antoniou—or the Gallery! If you ask me, your friend Johannes is as much to blame as anyone—he should know what he's risking when he paints such foolproof copies!'

Then she spoilt it all by bursting into tears. She didn't care what effect it had on him, until he spoke.

'Oh, for heaven's sake, *don't* cry!' He sounded exasperated. 'I can't stand women who cry—they always think they'll get what they want!'

'Well—I—don't!' she managed between sobs. And then added illogically, 'I wouldn't cry if you tortured me—I d-don't want anything . . . I just can't help it!' And she found herself crying harder than ever.

He looked at her in annoyance. 'Then stop it.'

'Why?' she sobbed defiantly. 'I'm tired, cold, hungry, I haven't got my passport or my clothes—and I'm not even rich enough to be worth kidnapping. So just tell me one good reason why I should!'

'Half of it is your own fault,' he said unsympathetically. 'But OK—because it embarrasses me.'

She looked at him through a blur of tears, brushing her cheeks with the back of one hand, surprised that he should admit it. And then she saw, incredibly, that he wasn't exactly grinning at her, but his expression had completely altered.

'You're—you're not in the least embarrassed—you actually think this is funny!' she choked, caught between misery and indignation.

'All right. So I'm not. It just happens I'm sexually susceptible.' The teasing note had changed a little. 'Every time I get my arms round a woman, I want to make love to her.'

There was a sudden silence. He was so unpredictable that she didn't know how to reply. And then the silence began to lengthen between them, and with every second she felt more ill at ease. He has to be joking! she told herself. He was watching her, but she could tell nothing from his expression.

'You said I wasn't your type!' she accused at last, tearfully.

'That's right—you're not. No,' he said, considering her, arms still folded, 'I'm not sure I even like you.'

He had made no move towards her, but the apparent detachment had a more disturbing effect on her than if he had put his arms round her.

Somewhere in the confused tangle this infuriating man had succeeded in making of her she sought for the shreds of self-control. She wiped her eyes, with a corner of the towel this time, and took a deep breath.

'I don't like you either, Mr Reissman,' she said, her voice only just a little uneven. 'There's a very simple solution to our problem, if only you could see it. We could be free of each other's company . . . very soon.'

Her attempt to regain some dignity was only a little spoilt by the fact that she had to sniff at the end of it. And she hadn't liked to add 'as soon as Monica gets back with my clothes', because she was no longer sure that Monica would come back at all.

He studied her critically. 'I, unfortunately, do not see the simple solution your way. There are paper handkerchiefs in the bathroom.'

She left the kitchen abruptly, and shut the bathroom door behind her. Then, despite her firmest resolutions, the whole humiliating situation swept over her again, and she cried in earnest. She knew he could probably hear her, and that when she came out her face would be blotched and her eyes red. And she would certainly have given herself a headache.

What on earth was she going to do? There was no hope of renewing the portrait negotiations now, and every other arrangement she had made was systematically being ruined by Caspar—unless he was prepared to let her go within the next few hours, which didn't seem at all likely. He still had her passport, and it didn't even look as though she was going to get her clothes.

Ringing the office wouldn't get her anywhere. Mr Geller might not be back for days, contacting Mr Antoniou was out of the question, Frieda was useless, and Alasdair Cullen—Geller's second-in-command—was also away for the weekend. Ring home? That would be more likely to cause worry than actually achieve anything. Perhaps she should have told Monica to contact Hugh ...? She imagined the Italian on one end of the line, and Hugh—cool, businesslike and polite—on the other, one eye on his watch and half his attention on one of his office minions. He didn't have much patience with dramatics or foreigners. He'd just dismiss her as part of some joke.

When she came out of the bathroom, she found Caspar sitting at the table on a stool that was far too high, helping himself to a crisp roll and English marmalade. He smiled at her in a normal, friendly fashion—ominous in itself after his previous veiled threats.

'There's another stool in the kitchen—you can sit on that if you want some breakfast. Pity Monica can't be persuaded to tell me where she sent the chairs. She thinks it's some sort of hold over me. Maybe you'd like to have a chat with her about it if she calls again. You seemed to get on very well. Coffee?'

She debated another haughty refusal, and then gave in. There was no point in making herself so feeble she wouldn't have the strength to run for it if the opportunity arose.

She accepted, with not very good grace, and fetched the second stool.

'And now,' he said, 'shall I tell you what your day's going to be like?' His manner made it clear that the plans were non-negotiable, and any remaining hopes she had of Monica's effective intervention evaporated.

'Please do,' she said, sunk in gloom. 'Just tell me one thing first—am I *ever* going to get out of here?'

'You don't imagine I'm enjoying this, do you?' The width of his grin belied the words. 'With you and Monica ganging up against me, what chance do I stand of bringing the criminals to book? It's your own fault if you've got to stay here longer than I intended—you've got rid of the evidence.'

'I'm not a criminal!'

'That remains to be seen, doesn't it? Have you booked your flight home?'

'Yes, for Sunday night from Milan. Which means——'

'Change it. You won't be able to see your dealer until Monday . . . if then. You'll have to ring London to let them know your arrangements didn't work out as expected, and you'll see them on Tuesday instead. That is, of course, assuming I haven't handed you over to the police by then.'

'But I can't stay here until Tuesday!' she exclaimed. 'They'll all believe it's an excuse to go sightseeing and I'll get the sack!'

'Oh, I'm sure you'll think of something. In about half an hour we're going to retrieve your bags and check out of your hotel, and then we're coming back here.'

'But I can't go out!' she protested. 'What am I going to wear?' She should have known better than to make a remark like that—it was an open invitation to him to give exactly the reaction she got.

The blue eyes looked her up and down lazily, and again he gave that unnerving impression he could see through every stitch she had on.

'What's the matter with your skirt?' He was making no effort to hide his enjoyment of the situation. 'It looked all right to me. And what's wrong with that very fetching creation you've got draped round you at the moment?'

She wasn't prepared to put up with the obvious sexual teasing in his tone. Thoroughly irritated with him, she snapped, 'Don't be ridiculous! I can't possibly go out in Monica's towel! She was supposed to be bringing me some clothes.'

She wouldn't have put it past him to have made his last remark only half in jest, but there was no point saving his ex-mistress's visit for a surprise attack now—if she was coming back at all.

'Why didn't you say so?' he remarked casually. 'It might account for the mysterious bag I got from her in the street.'

He got up to cross to the small lobby. There, in full view, was a brightly coloured carrier-bag with a boutique logo on it—just the sort of container Monica might have used to put her things in.

Bianca could have hit him.

On his way back to the table he proceeded to inspect the contents—a navy and cream checked skirt, some lacy bits of underwear, a make-up bag and a toothbrush.

'What did you think you were going to find?' she asked sarcastically. 'A shotgun?' And snatched them from him, her cheeks already fired with embarrassment. He'd made no effort to hide his interest in the wisps of lace.

He sat down again, and without haste helped himself to another roll and marmalade.

'Funny,' he commented. 'I didn't imagine you wearing sexy black underwear. I'd thought you'd have a pair of Victorian drawers under that artistically draped towel. What did happen to your skirt, by the way?'

Very definitely disliking the turn to the conversation, Bianca gathered up the folds of the towel in front of her and didn't deign to give a reply. Then she headed for the bathroom, praying fervently she wouldn't trip on the way.

She heard him laugh as she made her exit, and he called after her, 'You're just about the first woman in this apartment, Miss Bianca James, who hasn't been anxious to take her clothes off in front of me . . . What are you ashamed of?'

It was possible to slam the bathroom door very satisfactorily.

CHAPTER FOUR

IF ONLY he didn't look so disreputable! Bianca reflected with irritation, as they approached the smart, eminently respectable hotel she had found herself. Italians judged so much by appearances. He had changed to go out, and it seemed incredible that a painter could have so little sense of style and colour. If he had chosen the combination on purpose to create a hideous effect, he couldn't have done better. Caspar Reissman was a positive embarrassment. He was wearing an old pair of canvas shoes, a pair of shapeless trousers in an unpleasant shade of orange, and a pullover with paint smears on one sleeve. The fashionable blouson jacket he carried slung over one shoulder was obviously expensive, but totally out of keeping with the rest of his wardrobe. He was tall, unexpectedly athletic, and could even have been conventionally good-looking if he'd bothered to shave and comb his hair, but Bianca, her awareness of her own appearance very much heightened since she had become involved with Hugh and taken the job at the Gallery, felt mortified to be seen beside him. Especially in the context of retrieving her baggage from a room she hadn't used.

'I'll go in on my own,' she announced briskly, as they reached the entrance.

'No, you won't. I don't want you skipping off anywhere.' He still had his fingers at her elbow, as he had had all the way along the street—ready to grab her if she decided to make a bolt for it, she supposed. He was hardly touching her, but she had been uncomfortably aware of the contact every step of the way.

'How can I possibly "skip off" anywhere when you've still got my passport?' she demanded, aggrieved.

'I don't know—you might tell the management some totally unlikely story about my trying to rape you, or keep you locked up in a garret or something.'

'Yes. *Very* unlikely,' she said with heavy sarcasm.

'The first certainly is,' he replied ungallantly, eyeing her in that disconcerting way of his. 'And, in the second instance, I don't have a garret. But you're my only evidence now that you've so foolishly disposed of the picture.'

'Room No. 302,' she told the receptionist, trying to ignore the encumbrance at her elbow and persuade herself that it was nobody's business but her own whom she brought into the hotel, and whether or not she chose to use the room she had booked.

'What do you want the key for?' the Encumbrance demanded. 'You want to have your baggage brought down, and then you want to pay the bill.'

If she could have killed him with a look, he would have dropped there and then on the tiled floor of the reception area.

She smiled dazzlingly at the receptionist, and took the key from his hand.

'I'm going up to pack. You can wait for me here,' she said dismissively, hoping to indicate by her tone that her companion was just some insignificant bag-carrier whose life was in no way concerned with hers.

To her annoyance, he grasped her arm—rather too hard—and marched her towards the lift. It was impossible to resist him. He was far too strong.

'Let go!' she hissed.

' "Whither thou goest, I will go." You're my Naomi; I'm your Ruth. It's your own fault. Third floor, was it?' His mood seemed positively light-hearted. He was openly enjoying every moment of her discomfiture, and she had the unpleasant feeling that he knew exactly why she was so embarrassed.

Outside the door to the neat, clean, private and unslept-in room she had longed for last night, he took the key from her and fitted it into the lock.

'Tch, tch,' he commented, and shook his head in disapproval. 'What will the hotel staff think? Everyone from the chambermaid upwards will know that a Miss Bianca James—respectable, English, and prematurely middle-aged in her attitudes—didn't sleep in her own bed last night . . .'

Without a word she swept past him into the bedroom, but wasn't quite quick enough to slam the door in his face.

There was her bag, just as she had asked Monica to leave it—conspicuously re-packed and locked, just by the bed. Caspar took in the implications at a glance, that hateful look of private amusement in his eyes. 'So what was the packing story? A desperate bid to prevent the chambermaid from spreading the rumour of your debauchery elsewhere in Florence?' He sat down on the bed. 'Shall I rumple the sheets for you? Which side of the bed do you sleep on, the left or the right?'

She crossed to pick up her light, soft bag with its designer label, silently seething.

'Be careful!' he warned, making no attempt to hide his enjoyment of the situation. 'You get down there too quickly, and they won't believe a word of the packing. On the other hand, take a little bit too long and they'll think you brought me up here for very different reasons . . .' He sat down on the end of the bed next to her. '*Shall* I rumple the sheets for you? Or would you like to make the most of the situation—since your reputation is in ruins anyhow—and join me?'

He had deliberately goaded her past endurance, and she reacted without thought, her pent-up frustration getting the better of her—but the stinging slap she gave him proved to be a momentous mistake.

He caught her before she could get out of his reach, and with a forceful tug pulled her into his lap. She gave a little scream of fright, and perhaps if she hadn't tried to resist him nothing much more would have happened, but her immediate struggles only provoked him. Seizing her wrists in a powerful grip, he pushed her back on to the bed. Instantly she tried to twist away, kicking him, and then, gasping, found herself pinned under his weight. He was heavy, and so strong she could do nothing to free herself. With every muscle tensed in protest, she could feel the hard contours of his body against her, pressing her down into the bed. His eyes blazed down into hers, the colour of a hot summer sky.

'Quite a little wildcat under all the Victorian hair, aren't you?' His voice was unexpectedly quiet but its tone was almost menacing, and she shivered involuntarily. She was both furious and scared at once, and she didn't know what she could read in his eyes—their message baffled her.

'I wouldn't do that again if I were you . . .'

She tried to look away, but he moved quickly, grasping her wrists with one hand. Bruising fingers gripped her jaw, forcing her to meet his angry gaze.

There was a loaded silence—and, as she realised with a start of panic that she didn't know what he might be capable of, she licked her lips nervously. His eyes strayed to her mouth. She was aware of his hands on her tightening fractionally just before his mouth came down hard on hers.

She knew then why she had been reluctant to think about that first kiss on the balcony. Even though that had been an exhibition for someone else's benefit, and this was being done in sheer fury to punish her, their effects were the same. This time there was nothing gentle or teasing about what he was doing to her—it was almost savage—but she recognised the sudden racing of her pulse affecting her whole body in a way she had only experienced that once before, and there seemed to be no explanation for it—it was neither fear nor anger.

There was no explanation either for that strange tingling sensation that was taking over all her limbs, as though something was beginning to dissolve inside her—and she was no longer tensed to fight him off, but to resist this unaccountable effect he was having on her . . .

Then suddenly he broke away, breathing fast, and she

felt his weight shift as he rolled off her to sit up. Dazedly, she pushed herself up from the bed and straightened her clothes, flicking her hair back from her shoulders. She was half stunned, half ashamed—it had been brief, but if he had gone on she couldn't any longer have stopped herself from responding.

There was a tense silence between them, and it wasn't until he was examining in the mirrors of the lift the dull mark that was beginning to colour one cheek that Caspar raised a hand to rub the side of his face and broke the awkward strain.

He caught her eyes in the mirror. 'Not bad aim for such a spur-of-the-moment decision.' At least he didn't sound angry any more. The tension between them eased by just a fraction.

He made no offer to carry her bag on the way back to his flat, to which they returned immediately, without speaking. She didn't dare think about what had just happened, let alone risk a discussion on it. She didn't understand it—but she refused to feel guilty that someone other than Hugh had kissed her. She had made Caspar angry, but it wasn't her fault he had chosen to retaliate in that way.

Once back at the apartment, to give herself something to do, she cleared the table and washed up the breakfast things while he made a couple of phone-calls. One was carried on in rapid Italian; the other, in German, involved the name of his friend Johannes several times. At the end of it, he called to her in the kitchen.

'OK—your turn. Ring anyone you have to make arrangements with, and anybody you should have called last night to say sweet nothings to.' Was that a note of sarcasm in that last remark?

She stalked across to where he was lounging on the sofa and took the phone from him. Then she put it on the table and stood with her back to him, looking out of the balcony window. Since that episode in the hotel bedroom, she was intensely aware of him in a way that she hadn't been previously. It was almost as though it had switched them both on to another level. Now she was acutely conscious of his eyes on her as she dialled the number and waited.

'Antoniou Gallery?' Frieda sounded so close she could have been speaking to her in the same room.

It was crazy that such a feeling of relief should flood through her at the sound of a voice—and Frieda's, of all people's! But it established a contact with the sensible, everyday world she seemed to have left behind once she had reached the threshold of Caspar Reissman's flat.

'Frieda, it's me—Bianca.'

'Who? Oh—Bianca! I didn't think we'd be hearing from you—I thought you'd be off enjoying your freedom somewhere with one of those dishy Italians. How's Florence?'

'Awful.'

'What?'

'*Awesome.*'

'Oh. I thought you said something different. Is that you making that noise, or is there somebody else on the line?'

Bianca felt some of her confidence returning. There *was* another world—London, and the Gallery—and there were ordinary people like Frieda. Without looking in Caspar's direction, she said, 'I'm in a café and there's this peculiar man in the corner! It must be him. He's wearing the most horrible orange trousers you've ever seen and he keeps staring at me.'

'I bet he fancies you, that's why. I should get out of there as soon as you can——'

'I'm trying!' She felt mildly hysterical. 'It's easier said than done! Listen, Frieda, is Mr Geller there? Or Alasdair?'

'Old Joe won't be back for over a week. He's gone off chasing something he might be able to buy before it goes to the sale-rooms. And Alasdair's away for the weekend. Why?'

'It's just that—well—the appointments are a bit up the creek at this end. I haven't met Mr Pizzi yet. I think I'm going to have to change my flight to Tuesday. I'll have to ring again and let Alasdair know what's happening.'

Frieda giggled. 'I bet you're having a whale of a time
and don't want to come home!'

On the spur of the moment, Bianca turned to Caspar,
catching his eye, and said, 'Actually, Frieda, I've been
kidnapped by the portrait painter I came to see. He's
turned out to be a lunatic, and he's stolen my passport.
He's convinced the Matisse is a forgery and Antoniou's
is crooked, and he's forcing me to spend the rest of the
weekend at his flat.'

Casper was grinning at her, with no trace now of that
earlier, more dangerous mood. He made no attempt to
interrupt her.

Frieda burst out laughing on the other end of the line.
'Honestly, Bianca! One day that vivid imagination of
yours is going to get you into trouble—it's just as well Old
Joe isn't around to hear you or you'd probably get the
sack!' I'll probably get it anyway, Bianca thought
gloomily. 'Eek—someone's ringing on the other line.
Help—what do I do? I'll have to go, Bianca, I can't think
on two lines at once. No messages?'

'Only to Alasdair,' she said resignedly. 'I won't be back
till Tuesday—remember?'

She looked up to find her unpredictable kidnapper
studying her.

'If you're going to tell good holiday stories,' he said,
'you should at least keep them within the bounds of
reason.'

He had taken his shoes off, and was sitting cross-legged
in his shapeless baggy trousers on the sofa. Shirtcuffs now
flapped freely from the sleeves of his jersey, and the collar
stuck up behind his ear. His hair was once again an
untidy thatch and he still hadn't shaved. And this was
the man who, less than half an hour ago, had had her
pinned to a bed in a hotel bedroom she'd paid for and
never even slept in. Yes, she thought, for once I agree with
you. Truth is stranger than fiction in your case—I couldn't
possibly have made you up!

But the phoning session was followed by an

interrogation along the lines of the one the previous night.
The amusement she had seen in him during the call to
Frieda had vanished completely. As after Monica's visit,
he quickly succeeded in destroying her own sense of
humour, and the atmosphere became aggressively
charged once more. Within seconds she was hating him
again.

'I warn you,' he began, 'I'm better informed about some
things than I was yesterday. You've behaved very foolishly
in passing the painting on to your friend Mr Pizzi. I *know*
it's a forgery and I could make things difficult for you if
I felt like it.'

'How do you know?' she challenged him. 'Is this your
unrivalled knowledge of your friend's techniques still, or
do you have proof?'

He ignored the question, his eyes cold. 'You told me
last night you've worked at Antoniou's for six months.
How did you get the job in the first place?' he asked her
again, obviously well versed in interrogation methods.

'Through a friend of a friend, I told you.'

'Name?'

'What on earth does that matter?' she exploded. 'None
of this is any of your damn business!'

'In my book, *Miss James*, you're involved in passing off
my friend's copies as originals, and are therefore guilty
until proved innocent. Which makes it my damn
business. Name?'

She told him, angrily, and every tedious little detail she
could think of for good measure, until he stopped her.

'I think that just about sums up the London art world's
social scene, thank you. Had you worked in a gallery
before you got the job in Antoniou's?'

'No—nor had I taken a crash course in forgery
marketing for beginners.'

The long grim mouth didn't even quirk. He only laughs
at his own jokes, she thought. He's only amused when
he's making me squirm. Well, I'm not going to give him
that satisfaction!

He asked for details of her job, and the office

routine—how much contact she had with Joseph Geller and Alasdair Cullen, how much she knew of Mr Antoniou himself, and how much contact she had with clients.

'So,' he said at last, 'that brings us back to the painting again. When did you first see it?'

'Here,' she replied uncompromisingly. 'It was all wrapped up when I picked it up at the airport.' For one crazy moment she was tempted to invent some wild story—string him along for a while, and then show him how ridiculous he was being about the whole thing. But one more glance at that grim, unsmiling face killed the idea stone-dead. She couldn't risk provoking him to violence again.

'Who wrapped it? Who prepared the Customs and VAT papers?'

She shrugged vaguely and, seeing his quick frown, made more of an effort to concentrate. 'Frieda, I think. Some of it had been done earlier; we hadn't had it long, anyway. Things were in a bit of a muddle because Mr Geller was away at a sale and Alasdair was away, too, and it was just Frieda and me in charge. Frieda wasn't quite sure which paintings she was supposed to send on ahead, except yours. She knew a Matisse had to go to Pizzi, and she thought it was this one.'

'And who exactly were you delivering it to?'

'To whom,' she murmured without thinking.

The humourless expression did relax a little then. 'Quite a pedant, as well as a Pre-Raphaelite, aren't you?'

'No, I'm not! It just so happens that my Italian mother learned very correct English from my diplomat father, and passed it on to me.'

'Your father's in the Diplomatic Service?'

'He was. He died when I was eight.'

'Does your mother work?' There was something about the way he asked the question that suggested a more personal interest than before. Perhaps the eminent respectability of her father had affected his view of her.

'She's a writer—and she does interior design.' Why did

he need to know all this?

'So there's an artist of sorts in the family. And what about you, working for an art gallery—are you actually interested in what you do?'

'Of course I am!' The insulting implication—that she was working for the Gallery because she couldn't find anything better to do—caused her pale skin to flush with annoyance. She went on indignantly, 'I did an art history course at college. I mightn't know a lot about the business side of the Gallery yet, but I'd be pretty stupid if I couldn't learn!'

'No comment.'

She met his disconcerting stare directly, her own eyes bright with antagonism. There was another of those moments of brittle silence, and then they returned to the subject of Mr Pizzi. Most of the questions she couldn't answer. She wondered if he suspected her of being deliberately obstructive.

Finally she shook her head. 'It's hopeless,' she said. 'I can't make sense of what you're asking me. I've never even met Mr Pizzi—why don't you try Monica? She's had more direct contact with him than I have.'

'Very amusing,' he said sarcastically. 'At least I'm sure of Monica—she's too feather-brained to be criminally responsible for anything she gets involved in. I'm far from sure about you.'

'Thanks. But I don't think I care very much any more.' She was deliberately offhand. 'None of this is real—it's like a bad dream, and I'll wake up soon. Either that, or I'll lose my job for certain. So there's no point in worrying about it.' She stretched her arms behind her head, and closed her eyes. There was no point in arguing with him any longer, either.

'Why should you lose your job?' he asked slowly.

'Because I came here to persuade you to change the portrait of Mrs Brandt and to deliver the Matisse personally to Pizzi. I've not done either. So what do I care if I'm caught up in a forgery scandal? At least I can sell my story to the papers afterwards. They might even take me on as a Page Three girl.'

He gave a hoot of derisive laughter, and she opened
her eyes and glared at him.

'No, you couldn't,' he said. 'You're far too . . . skinny.'
The pause hinted that he had perhaps been about to use
some cruder term, and had thought better of it. 'If you
don't believe me about your . . . lack of qualifications . . .
come and look at one or two ladies who do qualify.'

'What?'

'Don't look so appalled. I was offering to show you my
studio. And that, I might add, is not an offer I make to
everyone.'

She looked at him doubtfully. Was this the Caspar
Reissman version of 'come and see my etchings'? So far
he'd made it pretty clear, verbally at least, that he wasn't
interested in her, but since the episode in the hotel
bedroom she wasn't so sure. She still couldn't make up
her mind exactly what had happened then, and she didn't
want to think about it. But, whatever it was, it had
happened because she had let her anger get the better of
her. Now his mood seemed to have changed, so maybe
she could afford to take the offer at face value.

Then she thought, why not? At least I'll have gained
something useful out of this—a guided tour round Caspar
Reissman's studio. She knew from Joseph Geller that he
never let anyone see him at work. She'd find out the
possible cost of the privilege later.

'Want a glass of wine?'

That definitely did sound like a preliminary to
etchings! 'No, thank you,' she said primly.

He raised his eyes to heaven in exaggerated patience,
and she knew that he was laughing at her again. 'My dear
girl, this is Italy! People drink wine at all times of the day.
As an accompaniment to talking, seeing paintings, eating,
watching television—even doing nothing. As well as what
you're thinking.'

'I wasn't——'

'You were. Would you like to see my studio or not?'

He opened the door and walked in, without waiting

for a reply. Her glimpse of the stacked canvases that morning had been tantalising. Now he was squatting down on his heels in front of them, leafing through them with the carelessness of a professional.

'The Page Three types are over there behind you,' he said. 'Have a look if you want.'

What followed was one of the first normal conversations Bianca had had with Caspar Reissman.

She bent down and sorted through the stack of paintings. They were all of nudes in various poses. Some of the canvases were no more than sketches; there were also drawings, and both charcoal and pastel studies. Even the most quickly executed of the sketches had the qualities of life and energy that were the hallmark of his work. She forgot all about her antagonism towards him.

'These are wonderful!' she exclaimed with genuine enthusiasm. 'Are they all recent?'

He came over to stand behind her, and again she felt that tingling sensation up and down her spine, and on the back of her neck, but she didn't step away.

'The one you're looking at is about eight years old. Some of them are dated on the back.' Then he bent down, and flipped through the stack quickly. 'Recognise this one?'

It was of a dark-haired young woman stretched out on a bed. The bed itself was merely suggested. The woman had her face turned away, and her hair spread over the pillow. One hip was provocatively curved. She had a superb body, and every line of her stated that she was fully aware of it.

No, she wouldn't have recognised her, but she guessed it had to be Monica.

She smiled. 'We've met.'

'That was in the days before she discovered henna. She's always trying to get me to sell this to her, but I rather like it, though it's not one of my best, technically speaking. Anyway, she's never got any money.'

'You wouldn't give it to her?' It seemed rather a mercenary attitude, in view of the relationship he had

had with her.

He laughed. 'I'd find myself buying it back at an inflated price every time she ran out of cash—or, worse, she'd sell it to someone else, and then I'd lose it completely. I'm fond of it, as I said, just as—heaven knows why—I'm still fond of Monica. This is part of our long-vanished past . . . ' He was looking at Bianca herself now, thoughtfully. Then he said slowly, 'You know, I've changed my mind about you a bit. Maybe I suddenly find Pre-Raphaelites more interesting. I'd quite like to paint you.'

'I wouldn't pose nude!' He really was incorrigible—this *was* all just a lead up to what she had suspected from the first—'etchings'!

'Wait till you're asked,' he retorted. 'Your body couldn't interest me less. All I want is your head. Believe me, I've had enough of girls offering themselves to me on that couch over there to put me off nudes—and sex—for a lifetime. I've had enough of bare bodies. A flip through those——' he gestured at the 'Page Threes' '—should tell you that. No, I just want your head, and your hair. And your yellow eyes.'

'They're not yellow!'

'Yes, they are. I've told you before. A sort of ochre colour with a touch of cadmium. Or maybe you'd prefer me to describe them in terms of peat pools, or bog water or certain kinds of cats?'

'You're hateful.' But for once she wasn't cross.

He chuckled gleefully. 'You sound just like Monica. Only she's better at punctuation—she'd have thrown something to finish off the sentence.'

'I don't want to be painted.' Again he was making her feel as though he had tied her in knots inside.

'OK. Suit yourself. At least that makes a change.'

He squatted down to replace the portrait of Monica, balancing on his heels. She studied him surreptitiously—the long sweep of those golden eyelashes was almost feminine from that angle, softening the strongly masculine lines of his face and making him

unexpectedly boyish all of a sudden. And his hair wasn't
really tow-coloured—more of a pale, silvery gold. It was
thick, and very fine. She hadn't really looked at him
before, just reacted to her very first impression of him.

There was something she was curious to ask. She
hesitated. 'Do ... do women really try to get you to paint
them by—offering you inducements?' Now she was the
one trying to find a delicate way of putting things!

His eyes, that innocent blue, looked up into hers. The
long mouth quirked.

'Oh, they do. They do ... And it's all true about artists
being lecherous—everything you've heard!' She
recognised the teasing note in that deep voice, but refused
to react, and he went on, 'But if I'm not interested in the
sitter—in artistic terms, I mean—I won't paint her no
matter what the "inducements".'

'What about Mrs Brandt?'

He stood up slowly, considering her, and again she
was aware of his height. 'A shrewd hit—you mean my
relationship with the Gallery was at stake? Actually, Mrs
Brandt, warts and all, has a very interesting face. Without
the warts, of course, she hasn't.'

'How do you mean?'

He took an unexpected step towards her, and she was
disconcerted by the sudden touch of the lean, artist's
fingers on the side of her face, forcing her to turn her
head towards the light.

'You, for instance,' he said. 'When I first saw you, there
seemed to be nothing in your face but a lot of attitudes
that didn't amount to very much.'

'And now you think you've found some warts?' she
said tartly. 'Thanks for the compliment!'

'A few.' He was still studying her, blue eyes half-hooded
in consideration under the shock of fair hair. His fingers
were cool and almost absently his thumb stroked the line
of her jaw, testing the flawless texture of her skin. Then
he took her head between his hands, running his fingers
back into her hair, holding her still. Inevitably, this
seemed to be a continuation of what had happened

between them earlier that morning, and a nervous pulse began to beat rapidly at the base of her throat. Did she or didn't she want it to happen? But his gaze was purely critical, objective, as though he were seeing her as nothing but coloured oils on a canvas.

'Yes . . . ' he said slowly. 'I would like to paint you . . . '

Then, as though his touch burned her, she stepped back abruptly, and his hands fell away from her.

'Do you paint anything apart from portraits?' she asked quickly, to cover her reaction. She wondered if he had been aware of it—too often he was able to read her with uncomfortable accuracy. But this time, if he had noticed anything, he didn't give a sign of it.

His answer to her question was casual, almost offhand. 'The odd landscape, but it's not really my thing.' He sorted through another stack of canvases. 'These are more respectable, if you want to look at them.' He took out one and held it up. 'This is my sister—one of them.'

The picture showed a young woman, about Bianca's age, very fair, with strong features. She had her brother's blue eyes, but the shape of her mouth was softer.

'I did that last year—that's Becky. This is my older sister, Caroline——'

The second woman, equally fair, wore her hair in plaits round her head, like a coronet. She was very pretty indeed, but looked determined. When Bianca remarked on it, he laughed.

'There's a will of steel inside that feminine exterior! Everyone is putty in her hands—including me.'

Bianca gave some consideration to the idea of the man beside her being putty in anyone's hands. It was hard to imagine.

'This is my mother.'

Again, there was a strong family resemblance—the fair hair and blue eyes—but Mrs Reissman looked more like her son than either of her daughters. She had the same mouth, but whereas his could look grim and forbidding, hers looked humorous. Bianca decided she would like her—Becky, too, but she wasn't so sure about Caroline.

She picked up a number of other paintings. He seemed happy to let her wander round as she felt like it, and sat down and watched her.

'What are you working on at the moment?'

'Another portrait,' he said. 'A local art dealer. I've only got as far as a few sketches. There's nothing much to see here. I go up to his house in the hills near Fiesole to work on him.' He had a pencil in his hand, and was sketching idly on a piece of paper as he spoke.

'Wasn't it usual for people to leave Florence in the summer months because of the plague, and head for the hills?' she asked.

'That's right. The city still gets unbearably hot. I usually go to Germany to stay with my family in July and August.'

'But I always thought you were English,' she said quickly. Then wondered if he'd resent the question; he seemed very keen on interrogating her, but he might not be so enthusiastic about giving any answers himself.

To her relief there was no veiled hostility in his reply.

'I am—my father was born a German, but he changed his nationality between the wars. My mother's German, and we have a vast German family, but I'm strictly an Englishman. Or perhaps an English half-breed, like you . . . which gives us something in common.' He gave her that unexpectedly friendly grin. 'How would you describe yourself?'

She returned the smile. 'I think you've put it quite well—only in my case one half usually gets the upper hand. Just at the moment, it's the Italian half—I always feel more Italian when I'm in Italy.'

She met that sparkling blue gaze, full of energy and humour, and for one second she stared at him, her eyes wide at the discovery of an unexpected harmony between them. Then she looked away hastily, and picked up another canvas.

'This landscape—why don't you think it's as good as your portraits?' She wasn't as interested as she tried to sound, but she needed to talk about something different. He had thrown her off balance again.

The canvas showed a typical view of a Tuscan hillside in spring. The light looked bright and new, and the branches of the trees were just touched with early blossom. He glanced at it. 'Oh, it's competent,' he said dismissively. 'It'd sell. But it's not a patch on my father's work. It's got nothing special.'

And the portraits had—she could see that at once. She had seen none of the sitters in life, except Monica, but she felt as though she would have known them anywhere if she'd met them.

Then something struck her about Caspar himself. She had thought him conceited at first—too smugly aware of his own reputation. But it was a reputation well earned, and there was no false pride about him. He was aware of his weaknesses, and was prepared to admit them.

She sat down carefully on a low stool, checking it first for oils. 'I'm not sure it would be very pleasant having one's portrait painted,' she remarked thoughtfully. 'The better the artist, the worse the experience.'

'What makes you think that?' His eyes were on whatever it was he was drawing.

'Because the artist can see all your faults. The whole process is too much about revealing character . . .'

'And is that what you're afraid of?' he asked quietly, glancing up.

'Isn't everyone?' she returned defensively. 'When you paint your sister, for example, what are you thinking about her?'

What she found really unnerving, although she didn't say it, was how much Caspar Reissman seemed to be able to see in the sitters he didn't know personally, and how quickly he could assess them—her, for instance. He'd got her all wrong about the business of the Matisse, but he'd made one or two very shrewd remarks about her in other ways. She hoped he wouldn't take offence at her own line of enquiry—there was still the business of Mrs Brandt, and she felt guilty about giving up on it.

The long mouth split into an amused grin at her question. 'It depends which sister. Becky talks all the

time—which I prefer. It means she's less self-conscious.
Caroline's like you—very aware of her image.'

'Why do you say that?' Why was he always criticising
her? Just when they seemed to be getting along better!

'Because it's true . . . ' He didn't look up. 'Everything
about you is calculated to convey a particular impression.
Shall I tell you the way you want me to see you?'

'Don't you think you've made that clear enough
already?'

'Have I?' His eyes met hers briefly. 'Then what is it?'

'Well . . . I——' She was embarrassed now that he had
challenged her directly. 'You . . . obviously don't like me.
You don't like my looks or my clothes, and you think I'm
a criminal . . . ' She tailed off, unwilling to go on in case
he suspected that underneath she was really looking for
his approval. And she had just made a rather horrifying
discovery—she *was*! Why she should care what he
thought of her she wasn't sure, but she very much wanted
him to think well of her, and for reasons which seemed
to have nothing to do with the Matisse.

'Let's leave the forgery business out of this for a while,
shall we?' he said. 'You haven't answered my question. I
asked about the way you wanted me to see you—which
is very different. First of all, I suppose you want me to
think you're attractive—and not just ordinarily attractive,
but something slightly unusual. Hence the Victorian
look.' His tone was completely matter-of-fact. 'The way
you dress is a compromise between the romantic and the
chic, and between the dated and the modern. Should I
deduce from that that your life is a bit of a compromise
too?'

She stared down, unseeing, at the picture in her hands,
and didn't answer. He was forcing her to face herself
critically, and she didn't want to give anything away.

'Then there's the way you act,' he went on relentlessly.
'You'd like people to think you're efficient and
businesslike—you wanted me to think that when you first
turned up here yesterday, and you were annoyed when
the circumstances didn't seem very favourable . . . '

So he hadn't missed a thing! She felt acutely uncomfortable—the object of some verbal dissection process.

'. . . Maybe you'd really like to believe you're one of the new superwomen—successful, hard-headed, and dynamite for any poor male who crosses your path, either in the business world, or in bed?'

'I don't believe that!' Instantly she felt herself blushing. He had surprised the reaction out of her; it wasn't what she had believed about herself—especially the bed bit—although there was some truth in the part about the businesslike image.

'Maybe not,' he replied coolly. 'But I think part of you would like to. So, if that doesn't fully account for it, what does? Who are you trying to please?'

In an attempt to hide her pique, she asked, 'If all that's only what I want people to think, what am I really like underneath?'

He studied her, pencil arrested on the block of paper he had balanced on one knee, suddenly thoughtful. That clear blue gaze was more than she could bear. She couldn't remain impassive under it, and stooped to put down the landscape.

'I don't know yet,' he said at last. 'But you're not as sure of yourself as you'd like to be, and underneath you're far too passionate to be a cool operator.'

She had to admit to herself that there was some truth in what he said. She could lose her temper much too quickly, and could let herself become caught up in her enthusiasms unwisely. Hugh was always warning her about it—it was something he didn't like in her . . . and Caspar had asked her who she was trying to please. She'd never looked at it that way before, but of course it was Hugh. She had assumed that because he was what she had wanted, they would automatically be right for each other from the first moment they met; but where she found that she didn't match up to his ideal she had tried to change.

Caspar was far too perceptive for her, and he baffled

her, so that there was no way she could retaliate in an attempt to analyse him. She reacted to him very often with strong dislike, but she could tell nothing of his character. She could never predict what would amuse him, or anger him, and she wasn't even sure if what she had interpreted as anger was the real thing. So far, he was a complete enigma. The careless, untidy exterior could be an 'eccentric artist' pose, or could be genuine, for all she knew. But one thing was certain: the sloppy outside was very misleading—there was nothing casual about his mental processes.

They had so far talked about images—the impression she wanted to create—and what her real character might be like, but what she found she really wanted to know was what he thought of her *now*—was there anything about her that he did like?

Prompted by a sudden overwhelming need to find out, she said hesitantly, 'When I told you what I thought your opinion of me was, you said it was wrong . . . What *do* you think?'

He knew at once what she was asking. She could tell by the little sideways smile he gave, and the way he looked at her. He put down the sketch he had been working on, its face to a pile of canvases stacked on the floor, and then got up, stretching, and looking down at her with a lazy smile. 'I didn't say it was wrong—I just pointed out that I'd asked you a different question.'

'Then I was right—you don't like anything about me?'

He was very close to her. Suddenly he reached out, taking one long curling strand of hair between his fingers. Again she was aware of that powerful effect his proximity could have on her, only this time it was overwhelming. Everything went out of her head, and she was conscious of nothing but the dizzying rush of blood through her body—but there was no fear in her reaction. She could scarcely breathe.

'Wrong again,' he said quietly. 'There's a lot I like about you, Bianca, when you stop pretending to be something you were never meant to be . . . ' As before, the palm of his hand touched the side of her face, his fingers slipping under her hair, but this time it was different. She knew he was seeing, not the face he'd like to paint—but her, twenty-three-year-old Bianca James who had turned up at his apartment on a routine job, and couldn't now hide the fact that she was shaking because he was touching her like that.

His eyes studied her, noting the winged lines of her dark brows, her small straight nose, the way her long, dark lashes shadowed her cheek when she tried to avoid that searching gaze. Finally, she knew he was looking at her mouth—and this time the tension between them became so acute she wished he would break it the only way that seemed possible . . . There was no question of a betrayal of Hugh in her mind—he never even entered her thoughts. What was happening here was out of time, in a world that didn't really exist, and her reactions to Caspar had nothing to do with her mind or her heart.

It wasn't until he spoke, coolly matter-of-fact, that she realised just how far she had entered into this dream world in which she wouldn't let herself believe.

'Shall we have a glass of wine now?'

Startled, she looked up and her eyes met his. He had withdrawn his hand, and unconsciously her fingers strayed to the side of her face where his palm had touched her cheek. She agreed to his suggestion without thought.

She followed him into the kitchen, and watched him take the glasses she had washed up earlier from the draining-board.

'What are you going to do about the Matisse?' she asked, after a long silence. It seemed a relatively harmless topic in comparison with what had just happened. Her existence with him in that flat was taking on more and more of the quality of that dream—she was beginning to wonder if she'd ever wake up. 'As you've lost the evidence,' she went on slowly, when he didn't answer, 'there's not much point in keeping me here any longer. Nobody's going to believe you unless you've actually got the thing to prove it.'

He was filling the glasses, and didn't look at her, but his words brought her back to earth.

'I'm working on it,' he said. 'I suspect that where that one came from, there'll be more to follow, though not necessarily through the same channels. I'm not sure I can afford to let you go yet, but, as I told you before, you've only got yourself to blame. Exactly how long were you going to stay in Florence?'

'A weekend . . . which you're wasting by the minute.'

Arms folded, he looked at her consideringly. 'All right. If you promise not to shout rape and kidnap too loudly, and you don't make a spectacle of yourself running away from me in the street, I'll take you out to lunch.'

'Thanks.' Her tone was heavy with sarcasm. The hint of teasing in his words had altered the atmosphere between them a little, and it seemed safer to return to the earlier, more hostile exchanges.

'Don't sound too enthusiastic,' he replied with similar irony.

'It's no very big deal when I don't see why I should be wasting my time here in the first place! I've already explained to you——'

'OK!' He cut her short. 'Don't let's go over that again. The offer of lunch is still open, despite your graceless response, but it you want to come out with me do change into some other clothes, there's a good girl. I'm embarrassed to be seen out with you like that. You look like the nineteenth-century answer to the Sloane Ranger.'

She stared at him incredulously, every last thread of that former curious tension between them now destroyed. '*You're* embarrassed to be seen out with *me*?' she squawked. 'Do you know what you looked like when we went to the hotel this morning—what you look like now?'

'Yes, of course I do.' He sounded almost smug. 'It took a lot of careful thinking out.'

He had done it deliberately . . .? She was so astounded that she couldn't think of a single suitable reply. Then, without quite knowing why, she began to laugh.

'You're incredible!' she said. 'Absolutely incredible!'

'So Monica used to tell me. Usually after a night in bed. But I don't want to boast.'

He had a way of making her regret her remarks, and the edge that kind of observation gave to the conversation was something it was safer to ignore.

He put a hand down inside the jacket he had flung over a stool, and held up her passport, flapping it at her.

'Remember!' he warned, and then scooped up the jacket. 'I'm going out for about half an hour to see someone on business—forgery business. If you're interested in lunch, get changed before I come back. *Ciao*.'

She pulled a face at him.

CHAPTER FIVE

LUNCH was a much more pleasant event than she had expected. They went to a snack bar a couple of streets away from the flat. There was a noisy coffee machine and the chairs scraped the tiled floor, where some young Italians played cards in one corner, with glasses of wine at their elbows.

They sat at a table near the door, and ate salad and pasta, and drank more wine. Several people came in who greeted Reissman, and Bianca was introduced to each as 'a friend'. The lie amused her. The fact that he seemed to have an extraordinary physical effect on her, and that he, at moments, seemed to find her attractive, didn't bear much relation to whether they liked each other or not. If the truth were known, she thought, she and Caspar Reissman would probably never be friends, and their relationship now might best be described as one of armed neutrality.

One man, introduced as Stephen, tall, middle-aged and darkly bearded, turned out to be another painter. He joined them at the table, and more wine appeared.

'Your first visit to Florence?' he asked Bianca, with a smile.

'No—I'm here . . . ' she hesitated deliberately ' . . . on business.' She looked directly across at Caspar and raised her eyebrows—it was up to him whether or not he wanted to elaborate on that. He was calling all the shots.

'Bianca's here to pick up some stuff for her gallery. She's staying with me for a couple of days.'

'Nice work if you can get it!' The deliberate ambiguity of Stephen's reply, and his eyes, told her unequivocally that he appreciated her looks, even if Caspar was critical.

She had changed her clothes while he was out of the flat, but only, she had told herself, because she didn't want to wear the ones she had slept in now that she had regained her baggage. It was chilly, and she didn't have a suitable jacket, but she had put on a thick, expensive sweater over her shirt, and a pair of well-cut trousers tucked into low boots. She had done nothing with her hair—if he didn't like it, too bad. Loose down her back it kept her warm!

Caspar had passed no comment when he saw her on his return to the flat, and she was relieved to see that he too had changed when they went out. The appalling canvas shoes and baggy trousers were gone, as was the sweater with the paint-marks and the hole, and he had actually shaved. He now looked casual—almost respectable—except for the untidy hair.

Lunch in the café gave her the curious illusion that she was no longer involved in any serious work, and that she was somehow on holiday. The meal was pleasant and leisurely, and both painters good conversationalists. They spoke mainly of the art world, and they included her easily. It made a change from being with Hugh's friends: they tended to ignore her completely, or made careful and rather patronising attempts to explain finance to her. She saw Caspar glance at her shrewdly once or twice when she was engaged in a lively discussion with Stephen. She had avoided using his first name, although he had used hers—it was something to do with keeping a clear perspective on the fiction that they were friends, and that she was voluntarily spending her time in his company. She wondered if he had noticed.

They returned to the flat by a circuitous route as a result of her heartfelt pleas to see some more of the city.

'After all,' she complained, 'I came here to enjoy a well-earned weekend break, apart from delivering the paintings, and the only thing I've seen since I arrived has been the inside of your apartment!'

They wandered along the banks of the Arno, and hung over bridges to watch the brown waters of the river flowing underneath. Bianca gazed into shop windows they passed, doing her best to forget about the fact that Caspar was *allowing* her to enjoy herself, until they were crossing the

Ponte Vecchio and she demanded a halt.

'All this may be everyday and boring for you,' she protested, 'but it's what I've come to see! Thanks to you, it's unlikely that I'll even have a job when I get home, so I want to buy some jewellery while I've got the chance.'

He gave her another of those considering looks.

'Don't buy it in these boutiques—they're a notorious tourist trap. Prices especially for rich Americans.'

'I know that, and I don't care!' she retorted. 'With you around to play prison warder I'm not going to get much of a chance to go anywhere else, am I?'

And she stalked away from him without waiting for a reply. If he chose to hail a passing policeman to assist in her recapture, let him!

The bridge was lined on both sides by a series of closely-packed little treasure houses, their windows sparkling with gold and silver trinkets, and she zigzagged from one to another, exclaiming at every new find. Caspar, after following her in the first few darts across the street and back again, took a leisurely course up the middle, pausing half-way to admire the view through the central arches of the old bridge.

'Well, have you found anything?' he asked finally.

'Nothing that wasn't wildly expensive,' she replied in depressed tones. 'You were quite right.'

'I usually am,' he said, with that smugness that she was beginning to suspect was all an act.

Her attempt at a flippant reply came out more tartly than she had meant. 'Why didn't you say so before?'

'Because you were so determined to ignore my good advice. Bianca?'

'What?'

'Let's call a truce for the afternoon. OK?'

It hadn't struck her until now that he was exactly the same height as Hugh—she had to look up at him at an identical angle. The blue eyes were deceptively angelic again under their thick fringe of gold lashes, but he wasn't smiling.

She had opened her mouth to argue, and then

something stopped her. Instead, rather awkwardly, she found herself agreeing.

'OK,' she said.

She returned to the flat with a couple of filigree brooches, and a pair of gold cuff-links for Hugh, the truce still—surprisingly—unbroken.

Caspar had been as good as his word, and had taken her to not one but several excellent little jewellers. Bianca had fallen in love with a silver necklace of individually linked flowers displayed in the window of the first one they had visited, but had been disappointed to discover that it had actually been sold already. It had been a one-off original by a young craftsman, and the jeweller had had nothing else like it.

Seeing her disappointment, Caspar had been prepared to take her on a hunt round the other boutiques, and had gone up in her estimation as a result. Except when he chose to annoy her deliberately, or regard her as a forger's accomplice, she was finding more in him that just the 'Horrible' of his nickname.

She cooked supper for them both that night, prompted to make the offer because it was better than sitting around hoping for a phone-call from someone, somewhere, that would signal her release from his custody. He hadn't mentioned her passport all afternoon.

'You can cook what you like,' he said, in response to her offer. 'Or is it a case of liking whatever you can cook?'

She gave him a glance she hoped was withering. To be fair, she hadn't yet revealed the fact that her mother was Carla James, the well-known cookery writer. She had inherited some of her mother's interest and flair, and supper was a mere bagatelle after organising elaborate dinner parties for Hugh—on top of a full day's work at the Gallery.

However, she said nothing of it to Caspar. It would seem too much like asking for his approval.

She wasn't used to having company in the kitchen while she prepared a meal, and tried to get rid of him.

'I want to make sure you're not poisoning me,' he said, a humorous challenge lurking somewhere in that blue gaze.

'Give me something to do. I can always be useful.'

'Haven't you got any work?'

'Not the kind you mean. No. I told you I don't have the sketches for the portrait I'm working on. Give me the carrots.'

She put a handful in front of him, and a sharp knife she found in a drawer. 'I ought to stick that in you and run away,' she commented, as he picked up the knife. 'Then I could have the weekend I was looking forward to, and go to the galleries and for walks in the gardens. Couldn't we come to some compromise? If I told you the name of whatever hotel it was I moved to, and promised not to leave without phoning you?'

'Regrettably, no. It's a tempting prospect to have the flat to myself, I'll admit—no you, no Monica—but if you really are in league with the Gallery you could just disappear. I wouldn't be able to contact you in London or anywhere else, and, as I said before, you're my only evidence.'

But however he phrased it, the implication was there—he still thought her guilty. There was a loaded silence, while Bianca cut up the meat ferociously.

Then he said, 'What do you do when you're at home?'

She glanced at him suspiciously. Was this a search for further incriminating 'evidence', or just a tactful attempt to change the subject?

'What do you mean "home" exactly?' she queried. 'Most of the time I live with two girlfriends in a house in Fulham. We pay rent for it but it belongs to Julia's father. Sometimes I go and stay with my mother. She lives in Richmond.'

'And what about this fiancé Monica says you have? Don't you want to live with him?'

She turned to face him accusingly, knife in hand. No matter what sort of an unreal world she had entered for the space of one crazy weekend, Hugh was strictly none of his business!

'When did you and Monica exchange all this information?'

'When I met her in the street. Very communicative, our Monica. Information not always to be relied on, though.

You do have a fiancé?'

'Yes.' She hoped the grudging monosyllable would deter him from further enquiries. She should have known better.

'And when are you getting married?'

'We haven't decided yet—not that it's any concern of yours!'

'Bianca, Bianca!' He gave an exaggerated sigh. 'I'm only asking out of polite interest.' He gestured vaguely, carrot in one hand, knife in the other. 'It seemed to me a perfectly socially acceptable question, but if you object to it I'll ask you one that isn't. Do you sleep with him?'

'That *definitely* isn't socially acceptable!'

He quite blatantly enjoyed catching her out.

'Which?' he demanded blandly. 'Sleeping with your fiancé or having an innocent voyeur's interest in it all? Want to know what I think?'

'No. And there's no such thing as an innocent voyeur.'

He was undeterred. 'I think all is not wonderful between you and Mr X. If it were, you would be married now, or at least living with him. Why were there no frantic phone messages left for you at the hotel last night? Why aren't you ringing him today?'

'Because we don't need to be ringing each other up every five minutes,' she said crossly. 'And he wouldn't like it if I called him at work for nothing. He has a very pressured job—he's a banker.' She wasn't altogether sure about the details of Hugh's job, but she felt it was a safe comment. She hoped he wouldn't ask for any specifics. He didn't.

'So when do you see this dynamic banker who has no time to hear love messages from Florence? You want these carrots? If the tomatoes need chopping, give them to me.'

She dumped them in front of him, wondering how to get him off the subject of Hugh.

'In the evenings after work. At weekends.'

'And do you stay the night with him?'

'You asked that before.' It was one thing for Monica to show an interest in her love life—after all, she had seen her as a rival—but why was Caspar so keen to find out?

'So I did. It all sounds a bit tame to me. Is it?'

'No. It's very romantic.'

He turned fully round on the stool to look at her. 'Romantic is just another word for Pre-Raphaelite in my vocabulary.'

She gave an exasperated sigh. 'Will you give those poor painters a rest? I'm tired of hearing about them! Tell me about Michaelangelo or Masaccio—you're an artist. You ought to know.' It was a topic that had occurred to her at random, but it seemed like a good way of steering him off her private life.

'OK,' he said agreeably. 'But if you've done the art history course you claim, you ought to know, too.' Then he proceeded to lecture her through most of the cooking process.

Once she found herself leaning across him quickly to turn down the setting on one of the electric rings.

'Caspar, stop tasting that! There won't be any left for supper.' It was the first time she'd used his name, and she had done it involuntarily. Well, so what? He called her Bianca. But it seemed to mark a new stage in their relationship.

He grinned at her, a friendly, likeable grin. With that sticking-out blond hair he looked as though his name ought to be Hans, and he should be in some German folk-tale. She had to repress the sudden ridiculous urge to run her fingers through it, smoothing it down to make it look respectable. He was even better-looking that she had thought at first—or perhaps she was just getting used to him. She found herself wondering what he would look like if he made an effort with his appearance . . .

On impulse she asked, 'How old are you?'

'Thirty,' he said without hesitation. 'I was telling you about the Medici sculptures.'

'Yes.' A little embarrassed by the trend her own thoughts had taken, she returned his grin. But she was still curious. 'I'm very grateful for the free lecture, but . . . aren't you rather young to be such a successful painter? Most people in your line don't make it for another ten or fifteen years.'

'Mmm. That's why I get photographed by pretentious

magazines, draped with lots of beautiful irrelevant girls. Because my father was a painter, I got switched on to art quite young. After that I was lucky—I had all the right contacts, and when my father died five years ago I inherited his mantle, so to speak. Now I'm head of the family.' He gazed down rather mournfully into his wine glass. 'I'm not very good at it, my mother tells me. My father would never have allowed Caroline to marry my brother-in-law—he'd have felt too sorry for Heinrich.'

'But isn't Caroline old enough to make up her own mind?' she asked, unable to keep the disapproval out of her voice. He had a very dictatorial view of his role.

He looked amused by her reaction. 'Oh, sure. Don't take everything I say too seriously—that's my mother's idea of my fraternal duties, not mine. She thinks Heinrich's very bad for Caroline, and vice versa. They bring out the worst aspect of each other's character, according to her—Caroline's love of bossing, and Heinrich's tendency to be a doormat. Her view is that if they don't divorce in the end, they'll be very unhappy.'

'That's dreadful!'

He shrugged. 'No one forced them into it. Caroline had some very definite ideas about the sort of person she wanted to marry, and Heinrich seemed to fit the bill. It happens. Sometimes couples have a way of suppressing the good in each other. Is that going to happen in your case?'

He was looking at her very directly, and she avoided his eye.

'Of course not,' she said defensively.

'So you'd say you and Mr X positively bring out the best in each other, then?'

She didn't want to think about any of the implications of what he was saying; they seemed like a direct threat to herself and Hugh—which was ridiculous. Surely his was a very pessimistic view?

'You were telling me about the Medici sculptures?' she prompted quickly.

He gave a half-smile, and took the hint without further discussion.

Later, over supper, they did return to more personal topics. The *boeuf en daube* had both looked and tasted all it should with the accompanying vegetables, and Caspar was warmly appreciative.

'You wouldn't like to move in, would you, while Monica's "out"? She's not a great one for the kitchen stove. I once had this naïve belief that all Italians could cook spaghetti.'

'Is Monica your mistress?' she asked, curiosity getting the better of discretion.

'Is Mr X your lover?'

Their eyes met in a direct challenge across the table.

'Yes,' she said. And then thought—that must be the wine talking!

'And—no,' replied Caspar decisively. 'I told you before. It's several years since she's been my girlfriend in that sense, and now we are, in the tried and true old cliché, just good friends. Monica might imagine every now and then she'd like to marry me—usually when somebody else has just chucked her—but what she's really looking for is a good, strong, macho Italian male who'll beat her up occasionally, and load her with fur coats and gold bracelets the rest of the time. You don't know anyone like that, do you?'

She shook her head, amused by this new view of Monica. She had wondered, in view of their allegiance, if she should try to plead Monica's cause.

'Pity,' he was saying. 'I'll have to try and find someone for her.'

'Did you give her that fur coat she has?' Now that he was in a mood to tell her about Monica, she couldn't resist making the most of it.

He shrugged. 'No. That was her last boyfriend but one. I happen to believe that furs are better running about in the fields on their original owners. She thought that was a sissy view—proof positive of my essential lack of male toughness.'

'You don't strike me as lacking male toughness . . . quite the opposite, in fact.' She saw the answering gleam in his eye, and instantly regretted her unguarded remark.

'Oh? What makes you think that?' His voice had that low, rather provocative drawl that spelled out an obvious sexual challenge. She tilted her chin defiantly, and looked at him across her wine glass.

'The way you resort to physical force when you want something!' That was even worse.

'How do you know?' he said slowly. 'I might want you ... but I haven't resorted to rape.'

She remembered the incident in the hotel—and then blushed scarlet. Maybe, after the way she reacted whenever he touched her, he thought he wouldn't have to ... She tried a different line of attack. 'If Monica wants a macho Italian male for a husband, what kind of woman do you want for a wife?'

'I don't,' he said shortly. 'Wives aren't my style.'

That went along with what Monica had told her, and it certainly didn't give him the right to make such pronouncements as he had earlier about other people's marital relationships. The change of tone was so marked that she felt that somehow she had scored a point.

'Where has Monica gone since you threw her out?'

He shrugged again, impatiently. 'Don't worry about her—she's got more brothers and sisters and cousins and aunts than a Gilbert and Sullivan opera. She invites herself to stay with me to get a rest from them.'

'Why did you throw her out?'

'She sold one of my paintings without . . . prior consultation.'

He refused to explain further, and the more open, friendly atmosphere that had been between them earlier seemed to have become tense. She wasn't sure why—perhaps he resented her questioning. Still, the information had given her an unexpected angle on his relationship with the Italian—she saw now that there were gaps in Monica's version, and if Caspar's statement was true then she couldn't blame him for evicting her. In fact, he had been remarkably long-suffering.

She mightn't have rung Hugh at all, if she hadn't felt the need to prove to Caspar not only that Mr X was a very real part of her life but also that his disparaging remarks about their relationship were mistaken. True, her parting with Hugh had lacked warmth, and he wouldn't expect to hear from her until she was back in London; she was counting on the cuff-links to help to mend things between them, but maybe a phone-call wasn't such a bad idea.

The knowledge that Caspar was there in the background would spur her on to make more of an effort—Hugh was very difficult to thaw when he was in one of his colder moods.

'Hugh Wells.' The curt, dry tones on the other end of the line almost prompted her to put the phone down there and then without a word, he sounded so forbidding.

'Hugh—it's me.'

There was silence, then, 'Bianca!' He sounded surprised. She had hoped he'd seem a little more pleased as well. 'What's the matter?'

'Nothing, darling. I just rang to say hello.' She didn't often call him darling. He was never lavish with endearments himself.

'Everything all right?'

Was she imagining it, or did he sound about one degree warmer? 'Fine.' There wasn't much point in telling him the truth about the Reissman situation over the phone.

'Deliver the paintings all right? No masked gunmen suddenly demanding them with menaces?'

'No, it was fine, really, darling. How are you? How's work?'

'Busy as usual.' He gave her a few sentences summarising the last couple of day's events, but she realised when he had finished that she wasn't much the wiser. 'Listen, I've got to go,' he said. 'I've got some people here——'

'Oh, who?'

He sounded vague. 'No one you've met. I really have to go now. Be good!'

'Aren't I always?'

'Bye.'

'Hugh . . .? You have forgiven me for the dinner-party thing, haven't you?'

'What? Oh, yes—listen, Bianca, we'll discuss this some other time.'

'Yes, of course.' She couldn't help sounding disappointed. She had the feeling he wasn't really listening to her. 'Bye.'

'See you.'

And that was the end of the conversation. It was just as well Caspar had disappeared into the studio. He wouldn't have been much impressed.

But her relief at his absence was short-lived. When he reappeared, he made a couple of calls of his own, one of them in German to his friend Johannes, and before he took himself off to bed, he delivered a parting shot.

'Feel like joining me tonight?'

'Where?' she asked, caught off guard.

'In bed—where else?' The wicked sparkle told her that he was, as usual, enjoying her embarrassment.

'Certainly not!' she said stiffly.

'Please yourself—I just thought you might appreciate a little comfort after your call to Mr X. It's not going to add very many lire to the phone bill, is it?' The 'comfort' he offered was deliberately ambiguous, but there was no doubt about the rest of the message. He was too astute by half.

Bianca, hating him with renewed vigour for drawing attention again to that awareness she had been trying to ignore all day, lay down on the sofa, doggedly determined to get a good night's sleep this time.

She lay awake for hours.

The following day would be Sunday. So far, she seemed to have achieved very little of what she had set out to do. She hadn't persuaded Caspar to change the portrait; they hadn't even discussed it again.

Then there was Pizzi and the Matisse, forgery or otherwise. She could only assume Monica had delivered it, as she had told Caspar, but she should never have let such a valuable painting out of her sight for one minute—let alone out of her hands! If the Gallery ever found out she'd get the sack straight away.

But why worry about that when she'd get the sack

anyway once any of the business about Caspar and the forgery came out! She'd have to ring Pizzi on Monday and think up some plausible story about Monica's connection with the Gallery, in case he ever thought to mention it in some future discussion with Antoniou's.

She would have to ring Monica, too, to make absolutely sure she would tell a sensible version of events if anyone ever asked her about the picture.

Then there was Caspar himself. He posed more questions than everything else put together. It was impossible to dislike him altogether. In fact, she did like some things about him—he had a good sense of humour, for example, when he wasn't directing it against her! Then he hadn't just left her to cook the supper, as Hugh would have done. She'd found that irritating to begin with, but in the end she'd rather enjoyed it. He'd helped her with the boring bits—he'd even done the washing-up afterwards—and then entertained her, when he wasn't trying to elicit information about her private life. His more disturbing comments on relationships, and the way he was constantly trying to provoke her, she decided to ignore.

So the real problem lay with the Matisse. If he was right about the forgery, then, although his virtual kidnapping of her was high-handed, it made a certain sort of sense. But what did he intend to do with her? He couldn't keep her there indefinitely. She'd have to go home on Tuesday, as she'd told Frieda, so he must make up his mind about her soon.

It was strange. They spent a lot of time arguing, but not about any of the vital issues. Was that just because he was good at sidetracking her? She thought about it, tossing and turning on the sofa. They had a curious see-saw relationship, the down bits dictated by his initial attitude towards her, and the high-handed way in which he was dealing with the problem of the Matisse. And the up bits? Well, she found him interesting, and his paintings, and his family, and his unpredictable ways . . .

What on earth was the matter with her? Only that morning she'd thought him insufferable!

Sunday turned out to be much more pleasant than she had expected, although she could contact neither Pizzi, nor Antoniou's in London, and despite the fact that ringing the number Caspar had given her elicited no response from Monica. The guilty need for reassurance that the Matisse had reached its destination made her jumpy and irritable, until finally Caspar proposed that they should go out and look at some of the sights she had intended to see.

He'd taken her first to lunch in a small, friendly restaurant, run by a family he seemed to know well, and then on an energetic walk up one of the hills overlooking the city to the Piazzale Michelangelo.

They'd stood leaning amicably over a stone balustrade that edged the high terrace, looking down on the city spread below them in the cold, bright sunshine. Caspar had identified the terracotta roofs for her. He could tell her much more about the buildings than she already knew, and she had to admit that she was benefiting from his companionship; it had been better than seeing the sights alone.

They'd gone on to San Miniato, its church decorated with a façade of coloured marbles, and he had made her drink one of the liqueurs brewed by the monks and sold outside in little bottles. It had a nasty taste, and he'd laughed when she'd pulled a face.

'A very satisfying un-Pre-Raphaelite expression!' he had approved. 'Florence is obviously good for you.'

'I thought we'd agreed to give that Brotherhood a rest!' she'd accused him with a grin.

'OK. Sorry.' Then he had added, 'It's just that with that hair you're a constant reminder.' He'd been standing beside her, looking down at her, eyes gleaming that astonishing blue and half hooded by heavy gold-lashed lids. He had slipped an arm round her shoulders, pulling her against him, and for one second she'd stood absolutely still in the circle of his arm, too startled by the sudden contact to make any reply.

Then he'd tweaked one long curling strand. 'Maybe you're turning into a very beautiful Botticelli?' And he'd let her go.

When she'd gathered her wits, she'd chased him down the steps of San Miniato, but was far too slow off the mark to catch him.

That curious moment was at the back of her mind as they prepared supper together again in the kitchen that night, Bianca insisting she did know how to cook pasta, even though she was only half-Italian. The teasing exchanges between them were becoming a way of skating over the unknown depths that such moments hinted at.

'Just because your ex-mistress didn't know tagliatelle from rigatoni!' she teased him. 'You'll have to choose more carefully next time.'

'Which—the pasta or the mistress?' One fair eyebrow was raised to punctuate the question. It was an expression she was beginning to find familiar—and attractive.

'The mistress, of course.'

'Oh, don't worry, I have!' he said with feeling.

She looked at him in surprise, eyes wide. 'I didn't know Monica had a successor—does she?'

'No. Not yet. And the successor doesn't know much about it, either, but she will . . .'

'Then how do you know she even wants to be your girlfriend?'

'She doesn't, but she will,' he said again. 'I have my methods.' And he refused to be drawn further on the subject.

She contented herself with the remark, 'You're very conceited, Caspar Reissman!' but he didn't rise to that either.

She decided to collect the items she was to take back to Antoniou's the following afternoon. Caspar seemed certain they would be safe in his flat, and he didn't argue when she asked if she could call the airport to arrange a flight home on Tuesday.

Then she rang Monica, before trying Pizzi. It would be as well to be certain of her facts about the delivery of the Matisse first.

'Of course I delivered it!' Monica assured her. 'And I

told the man I was your assistant, as you said. Where's
Caspar?' He was standing only a few feet from the phone,
and caught her eye warningly, but luckily Monica didn't
pause for an answer. She launched into a familiar
complaint about the *bastardo*, but, having heard some of
the *bastardo*'s version of the story, Bianca was now inclined
to be more charitable towards him. They agreed to meet
for coffee that afternoon.

For reasons of his own, Caspar offered to accompany
her to Pizzi's to collect the portfolio she was to take back
to Antoniou's. He even offered to take it back to the
apartment for her so that she could have more time to
spend with Monica. Having suffered agonies of remorse
for abandoning the Matisse, she was reluctant to let any
more Gallery articles out of her hands.

'It's not a question of not trusting you,' she argued. 'It's
a question of not doing my job!' Then she couldn't resist
the comment, 'You can hardly complain about my lack of
trust, the way you've behaved towards me!'

He just grinned.

But she was glad of his company when they got to the
dealer's.

Pizzi himself was not in his office, despite her
telephone-call. He was out, she was told by a heavily-built
man with shrewd eyes and a small moustache, to whom
she took an instant dislike. If ever there was a crook, it was
this one! Then she had to remind herself that appearances
weren't always the best guide—Caspar's, for example.

'You are not the young woman I dealt with the other
day,' he said, when she had introduced herself. They spoke
Italian, and he was looking at her with some distrust, his
manner curt and unfriendly.

'Monica was authorised to deliver the painting . . .' That
sounded official, but got over the difficulty that the only
authorisation was Bianca's. 'I spoke to Signor Pizzi earlier
on the phone. He is expecting me.'

'Signor Pizzi is out.' The reply was uncompromising.

'Will he be back later today? I could call again.'

'Not today.' The narrowed eyes darted from her to

Caspar and back again.

'But I fly to London tomorrow—the Gallery is expecting me. Can you ring Signor Pizzi? It's very important. If I could just speak——'

'He is unavailable. You have identification signed by Mr Antoniou?'

'No, but——' She was beginning to feel desperate. Frieda's letter was no good here.

'Then in Signor Pizzi's absence I cannot allow you to take the portfolio.' He studied her in silence. 'The other young woman who delivered the picture, was she from Antoniou's, too?'

It was highly unlikely that any gallery would pay for two flights to Italy when one person could do the job. The man was obviously suspicious, and complicated lies would only make the matter worse. She had feared all along that Monica would mean trouble.

She tried to explain Monica's errand as convincingly as she could, but getting through to him about the documents and portfolio Antoniou's were paying her to collect was like communicating with a brick wall. His manner was bordering on insolence, and she could cheerfully have slapped him. What was she going to do if he absolutely refused to hand them over? Her very first working trip abroad was proving an utter disaster in every respect . . .

'May I make a suggestion?'

The question, icily polite, caused even Pizzi's underling to react. In her agitation, Bianca had forgotten all about Caspar. She had never heard him use such a tone before, even when he had been at his most unpleasant with her.

He had been standing behind her, and now he took a step forward. 'Your name?'

Grudgingly, the man gave it—Rosso. Franco Rosso. There was a silence that Pizzi's assistant didn't seem to know how to break. He shifted uneasily under the clinical scrutiny of the other man.

When Caspar eventually spoke, the edge to his voice would have cut a diamond. 'Well, Signor Rosso—I suggest you put a call through to London as quickly as possible.

That way you can establish whether or not Miss James is authorised to represent Antoniou's, and we can all stop wasting our time.'

The long mouth arranged itself into a smile that was not a smile, and brought a look of displeasure to the dark face of the Italian—a look which openly said, Who the hell are you? But he didn't voice it.

'The lines—at this time of day . . .' Rosso left the sentence unfinished, and gestured dismissively.

Caspar moved towards the wide desk that occupied most of the office floor area. He reached for the phone and held out the receiver. 'Ring,' he said.

For a moment Bianca thought the Italian was going to refuse. He was wary, and resentful. In the absence, real or contrived, of Pizzi, he didn't know what to do. He was almost as tall as the artist, and far more heavily built, but there was something indefinable about Reissman himself that caused the other to back down.

Bianca, glancing at Caspar, saw that his eyes were completely cold. She was grateful that none of the contempt she read behind that look was directed at her. How could Monica, who had lived with him, ever have imagined he lacked toughness?

It didn't take long after that. A brief conversation with Alasdair Cullen cleared any doubts about Bianca's identity, and a sheaf of papers, together with a package was produced. Remembering the earlier fiasco with wrapped paintings, Bianca insisted on examining the package. She knew only that some drawings were involved, but she felt she had a point to make.

Rosso's manner had become more deferential since the phone-call, but he made no attempt to hide the fact that he couldn't wait to see the back of them both. It was a relief to get out of the dealer's office, into the street.

Caspar held out his hand for the wrapped portfolio.

'I'll take that back to the apartment while you go and have coffee with Monica,' he offered. 'Don't worry about it. I've got a safe in the flat where it can spend the night, although I'm not sure it wouldn't be better off disguised among the Page Threes on the floor of the studio!'

She smiled at him gratefully. 'Thanks for your help with that awful man. I should have thought of ringing London myself, only he made me so mad it never entered my head.'

He returned the smile, and again there was one of those pauses when it seemed to her that they were on the edge of something, only neither made the move that would take them over it.

Then, before she had time to say anything, he had taken the portfolio from her and was striding off down the street heading for the Oltrarno—the colourful district on the far bank of the river, in which he lived. Once he had gone, it occurred to her that now they both appeared to be on the same side he could let her have her passport back, and stop all the nonsense about keeping her in his flat.

Coffee with Monica was followed by an impromptu shopping expedition, this time for clothes. It wasn't the kind of shopping she could do very well in Caspar's company, and Monica's presence urged her to be more adventurous and try on things she wouldn't normally have thought suited her.

Caspar's former girlfriend threw herself into the enterprise with enthusiasm and, despite her own rather flamboyant dress style, showed that she had a good eye for what suited her companion.

They spent more than Bianca had originally intended on her Visa card. Then Monica accompanied her to Caspar's apartment, no doubt in the hopes of seeing the *bastardo* in person, but he had gone out. She stayed for more coffee and a gossip while Bianca unpacked her purchases, although the latter was reluctant to try them on in case Caspar came back in the middle of it.

There was still no sign of him an hour later, and Monica finally took her leave.

'Tell that two-faced rat I want all my bedclothes back when he lets you go!' she instructed. 'You're very welcome to them, *cara*, but he isn't! And you can tell him I've met a very handsome man called Marco who is taking me out to dinner tonight. I hope he turns green with jealousy.'

Bianca doubted that the news would have any effect at all on the callous *bastardo*, alias the two-faced rat, but she promised to pass it on.

They took an affectionate farewell of each other. It was unlikely they would meet again before Bianca left the following day—always assuming, of course, that the *bastardo* let her go.

She did give in to the temptation to try on some of her new things once Monica had left. It was making less of a parade of them, somehow. The only long mirror in the flat was in the studio, and that was where Caspar found her, pirouetting in front of it in a very stylish knitted two-piece Monica had persuaded her to buy. She wasn't even aware of his presence until she heard his voice.

'You've been spending money with Monica, I see!'

She froze. And then turned round slowly, her hair spread all over her shoulders, and embarrassment written plainly on her face at being caught so blatantly admiring herself.

Caspar was lounging in the doorway. He looked well entertained, but she was uncomfortably aware of the way he was eyeing her.

'Well, do you approve?' It was less a question than a defiance.

'A transformation,' he conceded, 'but there's still something missing.'

'What do you mean?' she asked defensively.

'The Italian look. You're only half-way there. Italian women wear more distinctive make-up——'

'I don't want to end up looking like Monica!'

'There's nothing wrong with Monica—she's extremely attractive. But you won't. Go and get your face-paint and we'll see what we can do.'

'No!' What on earth was he suggesting?

'Go on,' he said persuasively. 'What are you afraid of? I'm an artist, remember. I'm good at painting faces. Let me do it.'

He looked friendly, casual, detached, standing there with his arms folded. No possible threat. Why not let him try and see what would happen? It was all a sort of joke, really.

She went into the bathroom to fetch her make-up bag. I must be mad letting him do this, she told herself. No one would believe me if I told them!

When she returned, he had something that looked suspiciously like a tube of paint in his hand.

'It's Monica's,' he said in answer to her startled glance. 'I found it among my oils. She used to do her make-up in here because of the light.'

'And you didn't mind?' The glimpses of his past ménage with Monica were always unexpected.'

He shrugged. 'It seemed sensible to me. Sometimes I used to do it for her. Come and sit on this stool and let me put it on you—your face is the wrong colour for an Italian. Too much of the pale English rose.'

She refused to let him put on the tinted foundation, saying she would do it herself. It turned out to be an expensive brand of clear bronzing gel, and she used it sparingly. It gave her skin a slightly tanned, healthy sheen; an improvement, she had to admit, on the English winter pallor she'd had previously.

'Now let's see what you'd look like as an Italian woman,' he said. 'Sit there.' He drew up an old wooden chair, and sat astride it, facing her. Then he glanced at the make-up she'd left on the table.

'Very English,' he commented. 'But it doesn't always have to paint the same picture.'

He used her brushes artist-style, a look of concentration on his face. She might have been a canvas for all the notice he took of her as a person. She obeyed instructions to shut her eyes, and open her eyes, and turn her head one way and then the other.

When he started to paint her lips, she laughed.

'What's the matter? You'll mess it up.'

It was difficult to talk through the strokes of the paintbrush. 'You're tickling me!' she complained, and then the whole thing seemed so silly that she pulled away from him, helpless with laughter.

'Stop it,' he said sternly. 'I'm not giving up half-way through a masterpiece! You'll only have a beautiful mouth if you let me paint it.'

'What's wrong with it?' she demanded. 'I like it the way it is.'

He reached for a tissue, and began wiping off the lipstick. 'Stop talking.'

'At least it isn't mean like yours,' she said through the muffle of paper handkerchief.

'I haven't got a mean mouth.'

'Yes, you have. It's like a lizard's. Mean and cruel. In fact, as Monica said, it's the mouth of a bastard.'

'She didn't say anything of the sort!' He was examining his handiwork critically. 'If she'd made any remarks at all on the subject, they'd have been very different. Want me to prove it?'

His eyes met hers at that moment—that innocent, angelic blue—and she actually saw the spark of the idea enter them that was to change everything, and what had been a foolish game suddenly turned into something very different. He had been teasing her, and the suggestion had been made as a joke, but then they were again near that invisible edge, and she knew that this time they wouldn't back away from it. What was going to happen was inevitable—they had been on the brink too many times to draw back now. Her heart seemed to give an odd little flip, and her blood was racing with a strange new fire of anticipation.

Slowly, very slowly he bent towards her across the back of the chair. He put one finger under her chin to tilt it—and instead of backing away, as she should have done—as only twenty-four hours ago she *would* have done—breathlessly she found herself drawing towards him in complete surrender to whatever almost tangible force it was between them.

He gave her plenty of time to change her mind, his eyes holding hers until the last second—she read both a question, and his intention, in them. Then the golden lashes swept down and she closed her own eyes, as gently, very gently, he touched his mouth to hers. He merely brushed her lips, no more than that, slowly and repeatedly with his own, gradually inviting her response, but that strange fire now blazed up in a way that took possession of her entire body. It was so sudden, so utterly devastating in its effects, that she knew that they had both stepped irrevocably over that dangerous edge.

She found herself grasping the chair-back with shaking hands, seeking more eagerly the tantalising, intimate contact, while an unfamiliar weakness seemed to be melting her very bones. The impulse to draw closer and closer to him was irresistible.

Subtly his approach changed, and he began to tease her lips apart, the movement of his mouth on hers, and of his tongue, driving all sensible thought from her. Somewhere in the back of her mind she acknowledged that what she was experiencing was completely unfamiliar—never before had she known the desire to tantalise as she was tantalised, to make a man desire her so that ultimately, if she were to arouse him, and lose herself in the process, she could abandon herself utterly in the certainty that he was lost also.

Hugh had never made her feel like this. With him it was somehow all very controlled and polite, though she hadn't seen it that way before. Unsure that her uninhibited responses would please him, she was always afraid that if she let herself go too far he might—for some reason he would never have explained—disapprove of her.

But this was Caspar: the cynical, infuriating enigma she had been fighting with, in one way or another, since she had arrived in Florence—was it only three days ago? He challenged her, surprised her, and unexpectedly pleased her, and she knew instinctively that with him there would no longer be any inhibitions.

Then, even as the half-formed comparison between them came to her mind, she pushed it away. A voice inside her was telling her, This is crazy! It's only a kiss—it can't do this to you . . . And this is Caspar Reissman of all people! You haven't even the excuse of thinking you're in love with him . . .

But the new feelings he was evoking in her began to

claim her, and while she kept him waiting, enjoying the sensation that she was giving pleasure even while she was withholding it, her overwhelming instinct was to surrender herself to him. Then at last, unable to control that impulse any longer, she parted her lips to admit the intimate thrust of his tongue seeking hers, and her whole body responded to him. Heedless of the consequences, her arms round his neck, she pulled him towards her.

As though it was a signal he had been waiting for, he caught her under the arms and stood up, hooking the chair out of the way with his foot, and dragging her up with him, so that there was no longer anything separating them. His body was tense with the powerful urge he was trying to control. She felt his thigh between hers, and pressed herself against him, her fingers twisting in his hair. His hand slipped up her back, under the loose jersey top, sliding provocatively over her bare skin. The touch of his fingers sparked every nerve-ending, sending a charge through her that fired her and weakened her in the same instant.

The kiss deepened, and a compelling new urgency swept through them both. She wanted more of him, so much more . . . Involuntarily, a little moan escaped her, and immediately his arms tightened round her. But now that every inch of her seemed to be moulded against the strong, male contours of his body, the voice in her head said no!

Everything in her, even the hectic pumping of her blood, was arrested suddenly.

Then, gasping, she pulled herself away from him. She could scarcely breathe. His own breathing sounded ragged, and he looked down at her, his eyes strangely unfocused.

Her face was flushed, and her eyes very bright. They stared at each other; neither, it seemed, able to find words.

'OK,' he said at last, his voice sounding hoarse and uneven. 'So you have got a beautiful mouth . . .' He was studying her face. And then he gave the ghost of a grin. 'Now just tell me again I look like a lizard!'

The tension between them eased only by a fraction.

'But I didn't——' she began breathlessly. Then she hardly knew how to go on.

'I know what you said, Bianca,' he said softly. He had recovered some of his old assurance more quickly than she. His arms began to slide back round her. 'Want me to prove the opposite to you all over again?'

Despite her agitation, the temptation was almost overwhelming—never, never had she felt like this before—she couldn't understand what was happening to her. But a terrible feeling of guilt was beginning to wash over her, and that was something she understood only too well. How *could* she have done that to Hugh? Not only had she encouraged the kiss but, which was even worse, she wouldn't have stopped it if . . .

'Don't, Caspar—I'm almost a married woman!' Shakily she tried to joke. 'If only I'd known——' And then she couldn't go on. There was another silence.

'If you'd known what?' he prompted. He sounded tense.

'Nothing.' If I'd known it was going to make me see Hugh in that way, she was thinking, I'd never have let you touch me. Oh, what have I done?

With obvious reluctance he released her, and she forced herself to resist the impulse to catch him again in her arms. The silence lengthened once more, and she began to straighten her clothes. All the careless fun had disappeared with that kiss. She was in a turmoil. She didn't know what she'd expected, but it certainly hadn't been anything like that. Her body and mind were at war. She couldn't help feeling that something irrevocable had taken place, yet it was only a kiss.

Then, in an attempt to lighten the atmosphere between them, Caspar suggested, 'Why don't we go out and show off your new Italian looks? We could have a *cappuccino* somewhere, and then see a few pictures.'

She concentrated on clearing the make-up from the table. Her hands were shaking and she didn't meet his eye.

'Fine,' she agreed tonelessly. Going out was a good idea—they shouldn't stay in the apartment now. She made another effort to sound flippant. 'I think I'd like to see something old, and calm, and preferably very dead.'

She heard him laugh, but it sounded a little forced. She

couldn't look at him, and she was still acutely aware of that powerful masculine presence only a few feet away from her.

'Old and calm and dead,' he repeated. '*Va bene*. In that case we'll go to a museum.'

She put the make-up back in the bathroom, but when she returned to the studio he still hadn't moved.

'Bianca . . .'

She couldn't reply. There was something in the tone of his voice that made her almost afraid of what she was going to hear.

'You know I've changed my mind quite a lot about you, don't you?'

She didn't want him to say any more. It would only make it all so much worse. One silly kiss—and it seemed that it would rock the foundations of her life if she let it.

'Don't!' she said. 'I love Hugh and I'm going to marry him.' But even as she spoke the words she knew, deep down, that somehow they didn't ring true.

'Caspar—I can't stay here tonight—please let me go to a hotel!' Then she burst into tears.

CHAPTER SIX

SITTING in the office at Antoniou's, Bianca found it difficult
to believe she'd ever been out of it. Especially not to
Florence. And especially not with a mad portrait painter
called Caspar Reissman.

She looked across at Frieda, with her aristically untidy
frizz of apricot hair and her scarlet nails. She was chewing
the end of her pencil and frowning over her shorthand. It
was Friday—three whole days since she'd said goodbye to
Caspar on Florence station, and it felt like a lifetime.

She'd only seen Hugh once so far. They'd met, at her
suggestion, for lunch the day before. Their brief
meeting—Hugh was busy and had been distant and
preoccupied—had been unsatisfactory and disappointing.
Her own guilt since the episode in Caspar's studio had
made her tense, and their conversation had been stilted
and unnatural, but that hadn't completely accounted for
it.

She still had the cuff-links. It hadn't been the right
moment to give them to him. Perhaps she would find an
opportunity at the weekend, assuming, of course, he could
make it to her mother's for dinner on Saturday. He'd said
vaguely he was a bit tied up, and a sneaking feeling of relief
had added to that cloudy guilt hanging over her. Poor
Hugh. She still felt almost as though she'd been unfaithful
to him.

She sighed, and typed half a sentence of a letter
authorising the transfer of some money to a bank in
Geneva. Then her thoughts took off again, further south,
in the direction of Italy.

It was difficult to stop thinking about the way Caspar
had kissed her in his studio the day he had—literally—
painted her face. And then what had happened afterwards.

It was easy enough to tell herself now she'd been silly to cry, that she should have treated it all as if it didn't matter much—it wasn't as though she'd slept with the wretched man! But she would be deceiving herself if she didn't acknowledge that what had happened had changed her whole view of her life, forcing her to see that her ideal in reality lacked many, many things she was only just beginning to discover.

It was important now that Hugh should reassure her about that old vision of their future together; that it was not only still possible, but desirable. But he had been offhand ever since that stupid dinner party business. Was he actually avoiding her because of it? It was such a silly thing to get so out of proportion; she hadn't expected him to react like that at all.

That started her thinking about Caspar again: he was another who had behaved unexpectedly—especially when she had cried. After all, it wasn't the first occasion on which she'd done it, and he'd been nothing short of caustic the time before. She only had to conjure up an image of that untidy painter—tall, surprisingly athletic for all his seedy appearance, and now so dangerously attractive to her—to find herself back in Florence, reliving those few days that had been more real to her than anything in her life so far. Everything was filed in her memory like a filmstrip to be replayed at will. Everything . . .

'I'm sorry—I know you d-don't like women who cry,' she'd sobbed, wondering if, through the blur of tears, she'd be able to locate the source of the tissues he'd been using on her. He'd put one into her hand.

'I don't like women who cry to get things,' he said. 'Do you come into that category?'

'No—yes. I d-don't know . . .'

She resisted at first when she'd felt his arms slide round her, her body giving a treacherous little shiver.

'What's the matter, Bianca?' he asked gently. 'We haven't done anything so very dreadful. Is this because of the man you're going to marry?'

She nodded, unable to speak.

'Don't you think he might forgive you one kiss from an opportunistic stranger? He can't be up to much if he'd be jealous of that.'

She tried to tell him that wasn't the point, but ended up sobbing with her head on his shoulder. His arms were warm and comforting around her, and she wished they could stay like that indefinitely. And that only made it worse.

'Come on,' he said at last. 'You're spoiling my artistic efforts—I'm not taking you out anywhere if your face is striped.' But he didn't let her go.

She gave a watery smile. 'What makes you think you're going to be seen out with me at all unless you change out of that awful sweater you use as a paint rag?'

He laughed softly and kissed the top of her head, releasing her finally with obvious reluctance. 'OK,' he said. 'That's fair—you change your appearance for me, I change mine for you. But you don't know how much you're asking!'

He hadn't argued when she'd insisted on moving out of the apartment—he hadn't even discussed it—and he'd returned her passport. Taking her chin between thumb and forefinger, and tilting her head back so that he could look directly down into her eyes, he said quietly, 'I can't believe you're the criminal I first thought, no matter how hard I try.' And then the corner of his mouth had quirked into that lopsided grin. 'So since I can't stop you leaving tomorrow, although I'd like to—for other reasons—I think you'd better have this back.'

He put the passport in her hands then, careful not to touch her again, but she had to fight the desire to feel his arms round her, and somehow knew that if she made the slightest move towards him, they'd both be lost. It was a strange way to feel when they'd started off virtual enemies, but their relationship had undergone a disturbing change that afternoon.

They had dinner together in a small but exclusive restaurant some distance from the flat, and, remembering her early misgivings about taking him out to lunch, she almost wondered if she was going out with the same man.

Not only had he shaved, but, dressed in perfectly tailored light-coloured trousers and shirt and a navy sweater of fine wool that looked remarkably expensive, he appeared anything but the untidy painter of whom she had so disapproved on first acquaintance. His hair, that pale silver-gilt now that it was no longer full of dust, was thick and fine and had been well cut despite its former disguise.

Now that the subject of the Matisse was no longer a cause of major dissent between them, she tried to find out what he had discovered, but he refused to say more than that he had unofficially seen someone he knew in the police about it a couple of times, and had also contacted one or two dealers about Pizzi.

'It all depends on what Johannes can find out,' he said. 'It's not the only copy he's done for the original owner, a Dutchman called Jan van Heerlen. It might be possible to trace what's happened to the others. They were supposed to have been commissioned as keepsakes when van Heerlen got into financial difficulties. He found a source of ready cash in selling some of the family collection, but it's inconceivable that a copy should get on to the market without his knowledge—maybe he's trying to make his money twice over by selling the copy *and* the original in very hush-hush transactions through people like Pizzi. I'm afraid our dealer friend's reputation is not of the whitest.'

'Then you think Antoniou's must be crooked too?'

He smiled at her. 'Not necessarily. But we'll just have to wait and find out. Don't worry, Yellow Eyes!'

For the first time, the reference didn't irritate her. She just grinned and stuck out her tongue at him.

He booked her into a hotel near the Piazza della Republica, run by a friend of his, and delivered her in a taxi to the doorstep.

'You will tell me if you hear anything about the Matisse, won't you?' she asked anxiously, as they unloaded her bags.

'Of course,' he agreed. 'And the same goes for you—any information you pick up at Antoniou's could be useful. Ring me and reverse the charges.'

'Are we saying goodbye now?' There was a cold little

feeling of disappointment lurking somewhere inside her that she wouldn't be seeing him again after tonight. She couldn't have stayed at the apartment, not after what had happened between them, but she didn't want to see the last of him yet.

He kissed her on the cheek. 'No. Tomorrow morning at the station.'

Before she could say anything, he had disappeared through the hotel doors, and the taxi was driving away.

When she arrived at the station the following day and there was no sign of him, she thought he must have forgotten his last words to her. She was early, wanting to avoid a last-minute rush when she was responsible for the Gallery's property, but she couldn't help feeling a pang of disappointment that he wasn't there to see her off.

She thought then—not for the last time—about what had happened in his studio, trying to rationalise it. It hadn't been anything so very dreadful, as he had said. She had no need to feel so guilty about Hugh; she hadn't deliberately provoked what happened and Caspar had only been taking advantage of the situation. A kind of madness seemed to have come over her, and none of it could have meant anything serious to him. He was a self-confessed opportunist. The fact that she had responded as she had had been unfortunate, given the situation with Hugh, but not ultimately important. It was the man himself who mattered, not sex.

She had glanced at her watch. The Milan train was already waiting, although not scheduled to leave for another ten minutes. She hoped there would be no delays. It was important that she was in time for her flight if she was to get to London before they closed the Gallery. She didn't want the responsibility of the portfolio a moment longer than she could help. It would be as well to appear efficient in one respect of her job at least; she had taken two extra days, and had failed absolutely to negotiate the alterations to the formidable Mrs Brandt. Caspar had refused to enter into further discussion on the subject, even in his new and more amenable frame of mind, and she wasn't looking forward to her next meeting with Mr Geller.

At last she saw a tall, fair-haired figure striding towards her, coat flapping, through the crowd of Italians milling round the station entrance. Several of them turned to look after him as he made his way towards her, and she knew now that it was more than just his untidy appearance that drew their glances—there was something so assured and authoritative about his manner. She had seen him in a new light since the interview with Pizzi's unpleasant assistant.

'I'm surprised you had the nerve to turn up!' she challenged him, a little awkwardly. The thought of yesterday and all that had happened hung between them. She laughed nervously. 'I'll probably lose my job because of you—I've spent two unauthorised days here, got involved with a forgery that no one apart from you seems to know about, and now I've got to go back and tell the Gallery that you refused even to consider changing the portrait! I've been a spectacular failure.'

'Nonsense!' He grinned down at her, blue eyes alight with a mischievous sparkle, hands in the pockets of his coat, totally at his ease. 'I think you've coped with the situation quite well, all things considered. And if you lose your job, do you really mind?'

'Of course I mind!' she flashed at him, with more than a trace of the old spirit. 'It's my life—my future!'

'It just so happens I think you're in the wrong life, and the wrong future. If you lose your job, come back here and have lovely rows with me and Monica. There are things in you, Bianca James, that don't have much of a chance to get out in London.'

He must be teasing her, but there was something underneath it all that was more than a joke.

'Such as?' she demanded sceptically, determined not to let herself be surprised by him again. 'The desire to have lovely rows? Don't be ridiculous, Caspar!'

His mouth quirked to one side. 'What's made you so prickly today? You weren't like this last night. But I'll admit I am being ridiculous. Because you aren't going to lose your job.'

'How do you know?'

'I'm going to alter the unappealing Mrs B according to her specifications.'

'You . . . you *what*?' She was convinced she couldn't have heard right.

Caspar laughed. 'Now you can go back triumphant—only make sure they know how difficult I was to deal with. Then I can demand that the Gallery sends you here again because I won't negotiate with anyone else, and you can collect Mrs B.'

Impulsively she threw her arms round him, burying her face in the collar of his coat, laughing and hugging him at the same time. She hadn't realised until that moment quite how worried she'd been about Mr Geller's reception of her.

'Caspar—you darling! It's like—like Christmas and birthday rolled into one when I was about six! Oh, thank you—how can I possibly thank you?'

His arms were round her now, and he pulled her closer.

'I guess it's time to say goodbye before I start to make a few unwelcome suggestions.' Then, before she had a chance to ask what he meant, he was bending towards her, and his lips touched hers.

In that split second between her understanding of what he was going to do and the reality, she never intended anything more than passive acceptance of whatever sort of farewell he chose to give her. It couldn't—it *wouldn't* be a repetition of yesterday.

He didn't waste any time gauging her reception of him this time. His mouth moved expertly on hers, inviting her response, and that delicious warmth and excitement flooded through her before she could pull back.

She was conscious of the chill wind of early spring that was sweeping the platform, and the loud thrumming of an idling engine, and the voices of passengers calling one another, talking and laughing loudly as doors were shut. But more than that, as she slipped her hands under his coat she was aware of his arms tightening round her, and of how closely he was holding her, her body contoured against his. His skin smelled of a woody soap, and his clothes excitingly of paint and linseed oil—just as they had the first time he had kissed her on the balcony to annoy Monica. That warm weakness invaded her limbs once again, almost before she was aware of what he was doing to her.

But, as before, it was the thought of Hugh that finally broke the sensuous spell that was binding her. She tried to push herself away, turning her face aside quickly so that he could no longer take possession of her mouth. He kissed her cheek instead.

'Don't be angry,' he said disarmingly. But his subsequent words sounded hesitant. 'It's only my opportunism showing again. Monica's warned you about it . . . You'd better get on the train. It's going to leave.'

It was too late to say anything then. Not that she was sure what she could say—'I don't want you to kiss me like that' perhaps? It wasn't true, and her responses had signalled that to him all too clearly. Or 'You had no right to assume because of yesterday' . . .? But that wouldn't do either. He had just explained away the whole thing as sheer opportunism, and there wasn't much point in getting angry about that.

He helped her into the compartment with her baggage, and, because she had to say something, she said, 'Thank you for dinner last night, Caspar—and for all the guided tours.'

It sounded stilted, a bit 'Gallery manner', in fact, and she wasn't surprised when he commented, 'Don't slip back into the prunes and prisms now Monica's made a proper Italian of you!'

Then his lips brushed her cheek and he was gone.

There was no one else in the compartment, and she got up quickly to watch him from the carriage door—a tall, tousle-headed figure, coat flying, wearing a pair of trainers with his shapeless dull red trousers, and striding away down the platform. He was a total contrast to everything she had once thought she found attractive in men . . . things she was now beginning to see as very superficial.

Prunes and prisms . . . she repeated now, in Antoniou's

office. What he had been telling her, of course, was that she had adopted a very false image, in order to fit into a world in which she didn't really belong. She remembered suddenly, with a little shiver, what he had said about his sister Caroline—that she and her husband were not really suited because some couples had a way of suppressing the good in each other. Was that what happened between herself and Hugh? It was true that she had changed, in order to become what he wanted . . . Perhaps, if she let him, Caspar Reissman had the power to turn her world completely upside-down.

No. She wasn't going to let him, she told herself decisively, and typed one more word of her letter. Oh, blast Hugh! Why couldn't he have made an effort to be a bit more welcoming? If she hadn't felt so let down about him, that crazy painter would never even have crossed her mind again.

She forced herself to go on with the sentence: '. . . thirty thousand pounds sterling to our account with you . . .'

Frieda gave a heartfelt sigh.

'I hate Friday afternoons,' she complained. 'They go on forever. Are you seeing Hugh this weekend?'

Pushing Caspar very firmly to the back of her mind, Bianca allowed herself to be distracted by Frieda. She knew her enquiry wasn't a genuine one about Hugh, whom Frieda had met only once or twice when he had come to pick her up from work, so much as an opening to introduce the topic of her own boyfriend, Toby. They had little chance to gossip when Frieda's *bête noire* Old Joe was around. They didn't expect him back until Monday now—'Probably out on the razzle and charging it to expenses!' Frieda had commented when she'd relayed the news.

It was all very well for Frieda to joke, Bianca thought gloomily. She presumably knew nothing of the fact that Antoniou's had just passed on a forgery, which, however innocently, had been authenticated by the Gallery simply because it had handled the painting without spotting the fraud. She was almost convinced now that Caspar's assessment was correct, and the problem of the Matisse haunted her. Had the Gallery itself been defrauded? She knew nothing about the financial arrangements. There would be an appalling scandal, at the very least—and she would be right in the middle of it!

She switched her mind to Toby—a much safer subject for a Friday afternoon. Despite the fact that she had never seen him, Bianca felt that she knew him almost too well—nice, but indecisive. She was subjected to daily accounts in the ladies' washroom of the on-going saga of his relationship with Frieda.

But she liked Frieda and, because they didn't have much in common, good-naturedly resigned herself to the next episode of what she secretly described to Hugh as 'the office soap'. She hoped Alasdair would come in from the showrooms to interrupt them, or she'd have to stay behind at five-thirty to finish the letter.

She was spending the weekend with her mother in Richmond, where she was intending to entertain Hugh for dinner. Assuming, of course, that he wasn't too busy doing whatever it was—he hadn't been very specific.

'I can't promise anything,' he'd said, dark brows drawn together in a slight frown. 'There's a hell of a lot on at the moment—it's all this business of the changes in bank rate and the value of sterling on the international markets. You wouldn't understand it.'

Once she would have accepted a remark like that, assuming that Hugh was probably right—international finance was beyond her—but this time she had caught herself thinking, a little resentfully, 'Why wouldn't I understand it? I would if you took the trouble to explain it properly.' She'd remembered Caspar, and the small bar in which she had met his friend, the painter Stephen. It was her world they'd been talking about, of course, art and the art market, but they'd taken care to explain anything she might not have been familiar with, and they hadn't made her feel inadequate in the process.

But she hadn't given any hint of her new, surprisingly rebellious feelings. Her object was to get him to come to dinner, not to antagonise him.

'I'll give you a ring if I can't manage it,' he'd agreed in the end. And she had had to be content with that.

Carla James was petite, dark-haired and dynamic. Having been widowed early in her married life and left with one small girl to bring up, she had quickly looked round for means to supplement her considerably reduced income. She had assets—her house was one—but she didn't want to sell, and it wasn't long before she had turned one remarkable talent to account, and was producing a series of books on Italian cookery that had quickly established her as an authority on the subject.

Not content with that, she had turned her hand to interior decorating, and was now in the process of writing her third book on the subject of Italian interior design. The substantial royalties she earned had provided many holidays abroad for herself and Bianca, and frequent trips to Italy to visit relations at Christmas and in the summer.

Bianca adored her mother, and had inherited much of her spirit without quite the firm confidence in her own judgement and abilities that Carla possessed.

'So how was Florence?' Carla demanded, as they sat comfortably in the elegantly furnished room that had featured in several magazines as an example of her inimitable style.

Bianca took a sip of her gin and tonic and relaxed into her favourite armchair.

'Mind-blowing,' she said, 'but not for the reasons you might expect. I was lucky to have seen any of the art at all, in the circumstances.'

'I notice you went shopping!' her mother commented. 'Is this a new look, or a variation on the old one?'

'I'm not quite sure,' she replied thoughtfully. 'I met somebody who strongly disapproved of my appearance and saw it as his mission in life to change it—mostly by being rude about it.'

'*His* mission?' Carla's eyebrows shot up.

'Well, his ex-girlfriend saw it as her mission too, but she succeeded more by persuasion than insult. I'm not sure

Hugh likes it much, though—he didn't say anything, but
he gave me one or two odd looks when I met him for lunch
the other day. He's not keen on very obvious make-up . . .
what do you think?'

Her mother eyed her critically. 'I like it. And I like that
dress—it's got a lot of style. That shade of red suits you.
Hugh's just an old stick-in-the-mud.'

Bianca remembered her invitation. 'Oh, by the way, he's
coming to dinner tomorrow night if that's all right with
you?'

'No, he isn't. He called this afternoon to say he wouldn't
be able to make it.'

It wasn't so much the fact that he hadn't called her
directly at the Gallery that worried Bianca. 'Oh, no!
Mamma, you didn't let him know I hadn't even asked you
yet, did you? He's got this thing about me being inefficient
ever since I messed up that stupid dinner party
arrangement! His life's so organised he can't stand people
who don't get things together.'

'Hmph. I'm not as impressed as you are by Hugh's
organisation,' Carla replied with suitable emphasis. 'When
someone's life runs like clockwork the way his does, I begin
to wonder what they've got inside—lots of little wheels and
cogs, I shouldn't be surprised. And it's about time he forgot
all about that trivial episode.'

Bianca thought so too, but she wasn't going to criticise
him openly, even to her mother. 'But you didn't say
anything about tomorrow, did you?'

Carla leaned forward and patted her daughter's knee.
'Don't look so worried, darling. You can trust your old
mother to keep the flag of diplomacy flying. After all, it was
your father's stock-in-trade.' She got up and went towards
the kitchen. 'Come and help me dish up the supper, and
tell me a bit more about this portrait painter you went to
see. You said on the phone you'd persuaded him to change
Mrs Brandt for the better. He must have liked you a lot to
agree to that!'

'Well . . . yes . . . and no.'

All the way back to London, Bianca had wondered

about Caspar's reasons for agreeing to the changes, but maybe her mother was right—there was a simple answer ... Still, it didn't seem likely. He'd said he'd changed his mind about her, but that was over a very different question from the one of the portrait. But how could anyone explain Caspar Reissman?

At least, away from the office, she could tell her mother the story of the kidnap. But she found that just talking about him was almost a secret indulgence—it brought him back so vividly that she could have been reliving the whole experience, though there were a couple of episodes she thought it wise to leave out.

She was more disappointed than she liked to admit that Hugh had definitely cancelled their tentative arrangement for dinner. She couldn't help feeling he would have managed it if he'd tried hard enough. And, after all, he had known since before she left for Florence that she'd be there that weekend for him. Didn't he want to see her any more?

For reasons it was becoming increasingly painful to examine, it was vital for her to see him and be with him, either here at home, or in his flat just off Sloane Square. Because the more she was left to think about it on her own, the more doubts she was beginning to have about her future with Hugh; little niggling doubts that seemed so petty when she examined them that she was ashamed to have had them at all, but she couldn't dismiss them entirely. What was it Caspar had said? 'I think you're in the wrong life, and the wrong future ...' How could what had once seemed so right now seem so wrong? She didn't see how she herself could have changed so much in such a short time, and Hugh hadn't changed at all. In fact, he was so utterly predictable. Perhaps that was the trouble.

It had never seemed a fault to her until she had met Caspar. Then, without knowing anything about it, he had shown her a dozen little things that now appeared so unsatisfactory with Hugh—he never teased her the way Caspar did, or shared a silly joke with her.

Then there were the arguments. With Hugh every disagreement had been so tense that neither of them had ever said what they thought or felt, and there was always the sense of something unresolved afterwards. On the other hand, she had never felt madder with anyone in her life than with Caspar, but he'd proved so unexpectedly nice later on that in retrospect she'd almost enjoyed the rows.

And there were other things, too—the way he'd helped her in the kitchen, as though it were a matter of course, and the way he'd painted her face that day—never in a million years would Hugh have done anything like that! He would have felt that in some way it diminished his masculinity. Caspar didn't worry about such considerations—he didn't feel he had to prove anything. But then he didn't need to. His success was established, and he seemed to have no inhibitions.

She knew now that some of her early antagonism towards him had had a lot to do with the imagined threat from that self-assured, intensely male presence that had been an unwelcome challenge to her from the first moment of their meeting. But if he was a threat now it was not in any way she could have foreseen.

She found him intruding into her thoughts—tall, casually athletic, with those blazing blue eyes and untidy silver-gold hair, grinning at her, teasing her—whenever she was off guard. But what disturbed her far more was the all too real memory of the way he had kissed her, because until that moment there had only been Hugh, and if there had been aspects of their sexual relationship that hadn't been ideal, she had had nothing to tell her that it wasn't something she herself was doing wrong—some inadequacy, or unrealistic expectation in her, that made it less than it should have been.

And what made that even worse was the fact that she'd been to bed with Hugh, and she had truly believed that she was in love with him. Surely that should have been enough? And then one untidy, eccentric painter—a man she didn't even *like* at the time, for heaven's sake!—had kissed her over the back of a chair, and she had known instantly that nothing in all her relationship with the person she wanted to marry had ever equalled her experience in those few moments.

She tried to banish the problems of both Hugh and Caspar from her mind over the weekend. She watched television, and did some weeding in the garden among the crocuses and the thin green spears of the daffodils. Then she tried out a recipe her mother had been given, as part of the testing process they always went through to make sure that, when the dish finally appeared in a book, the steps would be clear and easy to follow. It was all very relaxed, in the typical manner of her home.

The office, however, was anything but relaxed when she got in on Monday morning.

'Watch out for Old Joe!' Frieda had warned her before she'd even got her coat off. 'He's like a bear with a sore head today. Something's gone wrong but I don't know what and he's going to take it out on everyone.'

Bianca instantly feared that whatever it was must have something to do with the Matisse deal. How much did he know about it—and what had he heard? She spent the whole morning wondering anxiously when the sky was going to fall on her. Finally she found out after a couple of carefully phrased questions to Alasdair—she didn't want to give away anything to him either—that the public cause of Old Joe's disquiet, at least, was his failure to secure the Paul Klee he was after in a Swiss auction.

'It had an unrealistically high reserve price on it,' Alasdair remarked cheerfully. 'What gets his goat is that it was probably all rigged anyway, and the painting was sold off to a rival. I'd steer clear of him for a while if I were you!'

But that wasn't possible. He wanted a report from her, in person, about her Florence visit, and then didn't know whether to be pleased or irritated by her triumph over the portrait of Mrs Brandt. So Hugh had been right in his assessment of her assignment—Geller had expected her to fail.

Still, he did have the grace to say, 'Mr Antoniou will be pleased. Mrs Brandt is very important to the Gallery—very.' And that was all she could expect in the way of praise.

His linking of the two names made her wonder if there

had been any truth in Caspar's speculations about Mrs Brandt's interest in the Gallery, but Geller was already asking. 'The portfolio you brought back—where is it? Frieda tells me you didn't return until Tuesday.'

He made it sound as though she'd taken a month instead of two days! She examined him covertly.

Joseph Geller had narrow-rimmed spectacles that should have been bifocals and weren't, so he was constantly pushing them up and down his large hooked nose. Bianca sometimes caught herself trying to predict the next movement to the nearest second. It tended to distract her from the gist of his conversation, which was hazardous—he wasn't, as Caspar had said, a man of many words. He had pale grey hair growing round the sides of a distinguished bald head, and he always wore pale grey suits. He looked far too respectable in every way to be a crook—unlike the greasy Franco Rosso—but then it was never safe to go by appearances, as she knew to her cost.

If the Matisse had been a fake—and she was more and more inclined to believe Caspar about it, since he had had no reason to make all that up, after all—then exactly how much did Mr Geller know about it? Or Alasdair?

Geller was waiting for an answer. She said something vague about not being able to see Mr Pizzi in person, and then something even vaguer about having to book her return flight late. Finally she suggested that he could regard the two days as part of her holiday quota for the year. That mollified him a little.

'We'll see. You've done quite well. I don't suppose Reissman gave you any idea when the portrait would be finished?'

'I didn't like to press him in case he changed his mind.'

'Quite so. Pack up that painting Alasdair sold on Friday, will you? The buyer will be calling to collect it this morning. And send Frieda in to take a letter.'

The week continued as it had begun, badly, but Alasdair's absence from Wednesday onwards with a bout of flu actually gave her an opportunity of watching her suspect boss much more closely. She was doing Alasdair's work as well as her own, which brought her into frequent contact with him. However, apart from the fact that he didn't seem to be able to trust her to do it adequately without checking up on her every ten minutes, thus wasting her time and his, there was nothing in the least suspicious about him.

Nervously, feeling like someone out of a spy thriller, she even took an opportunity to go through some of the correspondence files while he was out, but could find nothing even faintly incriminating.

When Alasdair came back half-way through the following week, Frieda was away, and Bianca now found herself working as Mr Geller's secretary—a job she hated. He always dictated too fast, and then changed his mind about the phrasing of earlier paragraphs. But she did manage to have a few words with Alasdair on the subject of her investigations. She liked Alasdair, a red-headed, cultured Scot in his middle thirties. He had a good sense of humour.

'Antoniou?' he queried, when she dropped a casual question about the general background of the Gallery's owner. 'What's the matter—afraid you'll be out of a job if the Gallery goes bust? It's not very likely. He's doing too well.'

'Then why is he worried about the awful Mrs Brandt?'

He shrugged. 'Oh, she did help him out a few times in the early days, I gather, but his interest in her now is probably nothing more sinister than ordinary gratitude. That painting was supposed to be a compliment. He just doesn't want to upset her.'

There was an enquiry from Mrs Brandt that very week about her portrait. The office air positively crackled with tension, and Bianca realised how jumpy she had got, living on the edge, as she saw it, of dangerous exposure—either of her own unorthodox handling of affairs in Florence, or of the whole fraudulent business of the Matisse which could land them all in prison.

'I'm surprised he doesn't stand to attention,' Alasdair murmured in her ear in passing. The unexpected aside caused her almost to leap out of her chair.

The state of nervous suspicion in which she had lived since her return from Italy was preying on her to such an extent that in the end she decided to ring Caspar. The temptation just to have a chat with him had been at the back of her mind for days, but now she had a legitimate excuse. There was no one else from whom she could find out anything about the forgery, and she couldn't stand the uncertainty any longer, she had to know what was going on.

She rang him from Fulham one evening. The call was brief but not for the reasons she had feared.

At the sound of his voice, that delicious prickling feeling his physical presence used to evoke in her flooded through her, and she sat down abruptly, weak at the knees, every thought of what she was going to say flying straight out of her head.

'Hello?' he said in English, clearly puzzled by the silence.

'Caspar . . . it's Bianca . . .'

'Bianca!' Did she dare interpret his tone as pleased surprise? 'Where are you?'

'In London . . . It's about the Matisse . . .' She tried to collect her wits. He sounded close enough to be in the next room.

'I was hoping you might be able to tell *me* something about that. How's the sleuthing?'

'I haven't found out anything useful,' she said nervously. 'But listen, Caspar, I can't bear the suspense any longer—I just can't trust anybody! I've even spied on Frieda when she's parcelling up paintings in case she isn't as innocent as she looks, and I know perfectly well she'd be useless as a criminal . . . What's going to happen? You must have heard something—I'm not going to find myself in prison, am I?'

It was reassuring to hear that familiar laugh. 'I wouldn't worry too much, if I were you. Most of the evidence so far points to van Heerlen and Pizzi as the villains. Antoniou's seems to be in the clear . . . But how are you? And how's Mr X?'

'I . . . fine,' she said quickly. She didn't want to have to discuss Hugh with him.

'Monica sends her love. Do you want a chat with her?'

It caused her a curious pang to discover that Monica was there—yet it didn't have to mean she had moved back into the flat with him. And what if she had, anyway? She had known all along it was what the Italian had wanted.

The conversation quickly came to an end after that. She gave some friendly messages for Monica, asked a few questions about what Caspar had been doing—not much, it seemed, from his rather bland replies—and reluctantly rang off.

It wasn't very comfortable to have to admit to herself afterwards that she would much rather have been in Florence with him at that moment than sitting about in Fulham waiting for Hugh to call—and that she was much more preoccupied by the thought of Monica being in Caspar's flat than she was by Hugh's silence.

She had met Hugh only once since their first meeting—again for lunch. It had seemed like an apology for not having had time to contact her.

'It's been tough just lately—lots happening on the international exchanges. The stock market's pretty lively. You know what it's like when I have to work late. We'll go out to dinner when things have eased off a bit.'

He hadn't said anything about missing her, or even *wanting* to be with her. But she had felt she had to make an effort to get things back on the old footing again.

'We haven't seen each other properly since I came back from Florence . . . couldn't we fix a date this week? Please?'

He'd given a rather tight, Hugh-ish smile, and topped up her wine glass—at least he'd bought her a good lunch.

'Don't nag, Bibi. We'll go out as soon as I've got an evening clear. My only free time this week's taken up by that do at the Southcotts'. Are you still going?'

Not 'we', she'd noticed, but 'you'. He was seeing her as separate from his life . . . Revenge for her cherished independence, or had he simply lost interest in her? Her whole existence seemed to be falling to pieces round her—first the threat to her job, now Hugh.

'What's happening to us, Hugh?' she had asked unhappily. 'Don't you want to see me any more?'

That hadn't pleased him. He was never keen on private discussions in public.

'This isn't the time or the place—we'll talk about it later.'

A sort of desperation had made her persistent. 'When?'

He had given her a hard look. 'After the Southcotts' do.' Then he'd changed the subject.

Seeing a suspicious sparkle in her eyes, which she'd tried hard to blink away, he'd relented a bit on parting and taken her in his arms in the street.

'See you on Friday evening, old girl. All right? We'll meet at the party. I'll have to go straight from the office.'

She had smiled and nodded, but when he had kissed her briefly she'd been aware of nothing but the chilling realisation that it was little more than an empty ritual between them. And since her encounter with Caspar she wondered whether it had ever been very much more than that . . .

CHAPTER SEVEN

THE Southcotts' party, instead of clearing up matters between Bianca and Hugh, only made things worse.

He spent the first half-hour in her company, but when they drifted apart later on it took her a while to track him down. She eventually found him in the conservatory, talking to a business friend.

'Can't we go somewhere for supper, Hugh—now, tonight?' she asked when they were at last alone. It was vital to her that they talked things out—she was living in a kind of limbo, with nothing certain, either her job or her private life.

Hugh was still wearing his City clothes, and he looked, as always, tall and distinguished. But for the first time it failed to impress her. You didn't have to wear a hand-tailored suit to turn people's heads—she knew someone who could dress like a tramp and still project that powerful aura of authority.

'I'm sorry, Bibi. I can't tonight. Something's come up since I saw you last. I've got to go on to dinner with Simon. We're meeting a couple of people—unofficial business. You'd be bored. It's fairly heavy stuff. Come round to the flat some time next week for a meal. We'll talk then.'

The message was clear. If he'd really wanted to see her, and the meeting was urgent, he'd have taken her along to dinner, too. It wasn't as though Simon was a stranger. But she was shocked to find that she wasn't even disappointed ... Yes, she would be bored—she had been bored at every business dinner she had been to. It was only the magic of Hugh's presence that had drawn her there, making it somehow worthwhile. And now there was no magic any longer ... for either of them, it seemed. But she had to be sure.

'When?' she asked, trying to force him into a firm
commitment.

'I'll ring you. Look, I have to go. I can't keep Simon
waiting.' He leaned towards her, to give her a peck on the
cheek, a perfunctory goodbye kiss as though she were any
casual friend.

The very thing she was trying to prevent had already
happened—there was a hole in their relationship a mile
wide. Why am I trying so hard with this? she asked herself
bleakly. There's nothing left to mend. It had been obvious
for the last three weeks that he hadn't been keen to see her,
but she had been so caught up in her own feelings of guilt
over Caspar that she hadn't been able to see it, blaming
herself for their estrangement as a sort of punishment.

She wondered what he would have done if she had
caught him in her arms and forced him to kiss her properly.
But it wouldn't have made much difference. She knew now
there had never been any real fire between herself and
Hugh, only a sort of airy romanticism.

Someone came into the room, and Hugh was gone. She
left soon afterwards—a party was the last place she wanted
to be—to find Hugh still on his way out. He was with Simon
and another man, and there was a girl with them. She was
a blonde with pale, English, porcelain skin, and perfect
clothes. Bianca vaguely remembered having been
introduced to her somewhere—her name was Charlotte.
She half wondered why she should be with them—perhaps
they were giving her a lift. Then she forgot about her.

She made her farewells in a kind of daze, and got into
her car, to drive back to Fulham as though on autopilot.
All the time she was aware that the old pattern of her life
was falling to pieces. Everything she had thought she
believed in had proved false. She and Hugh had no future
together any more, and he didn't have the courage to admit
it.

Even talking a couple of customers into buying one of the
most expensive exhibits in the Gallery didn't cheer her up
after that. What was the point of doing well in your job,

when tomorrow you mightn't have a job to go to? Any optimism she had felt as a result of her call to Caspar had faded—and again she found herself assessing her colleagues daily as potential crooks.

But since the party her moods had been very much affected by what seemed to have happened with Hugh. Again and again she asked herself whether she wasn't over-interpreting what was just an ordinary work crisis in his life, and then couldn't be sure how she'd feel if that turned out to be true.

She tried not to think of Caspar too often. Indulging a tendency to dream about him was far too dangerous.

She wasn't prepared for anything out of the ordinary the day Frieda burst into the tiny office they both shared with Alasdair and announced excitedly, 'There's the most gorgeous man in the showrooms—and he wants to see you!'

Bianca's heart gave a curious little flip, but the only feeling she could identify was one of dismay. 'You mean it's Hugh?' Had he decided he wanted to go on seeing her after all?

'No—not Hugh, silly. This one's tall and blond and German-looking, but he must be English because he doesn't speak like a foreigner and he's got the most sexy voice!' Frieda took a breath. 'He says he knows you're in here, and he's going to come in and fetch you if you don't go out there at once!'

Frieda was thrilled by the masterful nature of the mysterious stranger—he was the Toby of her dreams.

For no good reason Bianca felt as though her bones had suddenly turned to water.

'Oh, and he said did we have any Pre-Raphaelite paintings? I said I didn't know, and we don't, Bianca, do we?'

Bianca wasn't listening. She was almost as breathless as Frieda, but with feelings so unexpected she didn't know quite how she was going to get from the desk to the door, let alone walk coolly out into the showrooms.

There were only a couple of customers. One of them

was standing with his back to her, looking at some of the
carefully hung works, hands in the pockets of a dark,
elegantly tailored overcoat. For one moment she didn't
recognise him. In her mind she had pictured him as she
had last seen him, and this new image was so unexpected
she had almost dismissed him as just another buyer when
he turned to face her.

It was Caspar Reissman all right, but a totally unfamiliar
Caspar. Frieda's unlikely account hadn't been so
inaccurate, after all. When he turned to face her, he looked
more formidable in the dark, well-cut business clothes than
she had ever seen him. He was almost a stranger. Then he
gave a familiar grin.

'I'm looking for a Burne-Jones,' he said. 'I heard
Antoniou's had a beautiful one, but it seems the subject's
been too much influenced by the Italian to be convincingly
genuine?'

'Caspar!' She wanted to throw her arms round his neck
in her delight at seeing him, but with Alasdair talking to a
buyer only a few yards away, and Frieda watching
goggle-eyed from the office doorway, it seemed like a bad
idea.

Caspar wasn't much inhibited, though. He kissed her
enthusiastically on both cheeks, and tilted her chin so that
she had to look him in the eyes.

'Still yellow,' he said. 'I was right—ochre with a touch of
cadmium. How's the banker? Married yet?'

She looked round in embarrassment. No one except
Frieda was taking much notice.

'Sssh! No. We can't talk here——'

He took hold of her left hand, and held it up, examining
it.

'No ring?'

'Caspar!' She was agonised. 'We're—I told you . . . have
you come to buy something?'

He still had hold of her hand. She tried to draw it away,
but he wasn't going to let go.

'No.' That blue, angelic look she had come to mistrust
was in his eyes. 'To steal. You. I thought we might have

lunch together.'

'But it's only half-past eleven!'

'Ever been kidnapped?'

There was such an obvious double edge to the question that she blushed. Frieda was agog.

'Let's go!' she said desperately. And then, to the gaping Frieda, she added, 'This is Caspar Reissman—the portrait painter I went to see in Florence——' Frieda looked utterly blank, then startled.

'Oh . . .!' she breathed, embarrassingly impressed after her momentary lapse.

Bianca snatched back her fingers the moment Caspar released them to shake hands with Frieda, and made for the door. 'I'm going to get my coat——'

It was just as well Old Joe was out for the day.

Once they were outside, he took her hand again, tucking it into the crook of his arm. She was feeling absurdly pleased to see him. Her feet didn't seem to be touching the ground. This is ridiculous, she kept telling herself. He must be here on business—he hasn't come to see me!

'Are you here about the Matisse?' she asked eagerly. 'I've hardly been able to sleep a wink since Florence! Don't you know anything about what's going on?'

He gave the familiar quirky grin. 'Stop worrying. I'll tell you the news later—it's nothing dramatic, and it's got nothing to do with my being over here.'

'What are you here for, then?' She hoped he wouldn't guess what she was wanting him to say.

'Seeing my bank manager, seeing the agent who handles my property lets for me, seeing the tenants who were causing me a lot of hassle . . . among other things.'

'Oh.' And then, 'I didn't know you had a house in England?'

'Two, in fact—in London. My father bought them in the early thirties when he applied for British citizenship. They're worth an absolute fortune now, and they're part of the reason I could afford to embark on the career of a layabout painter.' But as usual he hadn't missed a thing. 'What were you hoping I'd say—that I'd come to see you?'

She decided to brazen it out. 'Of course! You mean to say you haven't?'

He stopped dead in the street, and pulled her round to look down at her. The intensity in those brilliant blue eyes almost took her breath away.

'How's Mr X?'

The smile froze on Bianca's face. 'He's . . . it's—I'll tell you later.'

But Caspar was no Hugh, to observe the constraints of time or place—as he traced the side of her jaw with a forefinger, and then a line across her lips, he created instantly a private world, light-years away from the jostling life of the street. The tantalising feather-touch instantly had its effect, and she longed for him to kiss her properly—and then thought better of it. With him her body always reacted too quickly, before her mind had had time to catch up. She pulled away, and started to walk again, saying the first thing that occurred to her.

'What's happened to Mrs Brandt's portrait—have you brought it with you?'

'I told you I'd get Antoniou's to send you out to Florence for it, didn't I?' She'd forgotten how seductive just that deep, attractive voice could be. 'There ought to be some Italian business coming their way before too long, and we'll arrange another quick trip for you . . . It really is a bit early for lunch, isn't it? Shall we go for a walk by the Tower?'

She laughed at the unexpected suggestion, but she was so pleased to be with him again that she was happy to do whatever he wanted.

It was cold when they reached the river and the sky was full of racing grey clouds. The Thames looked grey, and the Tower looked grey. Only the daffodils in the flowerbeds provided any splash of colour for the chill spring day.

'Are you sure you want this?' she asked, shivering. 'Couldn't we go inside and look at the Beefeaters if you're so keen on doing the tourist stunt?'

'Fine,' he agreed. 'But I'm not doing this as a tourist—I was brought up in England. I come back a couple of times every year for my English "fix". I love Florence—I wouldn't

want to live anywhere else—but this is my country, and for
me the Tower is one of the places that sums it all up.'

'What made your father change his nationality?' she
asked, curious to know more of his background. 'It's a big
step.'

They were walking slowly along by the river. White gulls
tossed overhead, and a boat chugged downstream under
Tower Bridge.

'He'd been to school in England, and I think he felt more
at home here than in his own country. And then he got
hooked on the cricket, like me!'

She looked at him sideways, the wind ruffling her long
hair.

'I didn't imagine you as a cricketer.'

He grinned. 'I'm not. I used to play at school—I was
Captain of the First Eleven in those days. But being a
painter doesn't leave much time for sport. I go jogging along
the Arno at night instead. Except when I'm taking beautiful
half-Italians out to dinner . . .'

She ignored the implications. 'I always imagine you
sitting about in bars near the Ponte Vecchio with people
like Stephen, drinking and talking all night.'

'I'm glad you *always imagine me*,' he said, stopping so
that she was pulled to a halt, too, by his hand on her arm.
'That means you can't stop thinking about me . . . just as I
can't stop thinking about you.' His voice had deepened,
and his fingers bit into her flesh even through
the sleeve of her coat.

She refused to let him force her round to face him, and
lowered her head quickly, letting her hair hide her
expression as she pretended to look down into the river.
Her heart was pounding so loudly she thought he must
hear it. She put out a hand to the parapet to steady
herself—she felt so dizzy there were motes of light floating
before her eyes.

'Bianca——' he said roughly, 'this man you're involved
with. Does he still want to marry you? I've got to know.'

She shook her head, trying to breathe evenly. She didn't
want her voice to betray the inexplicable turmoil of

emotions inside her.

'I'm not sure,' she said at last, so low he had to bend to catch the words. 'I'm just not sure about anything any longer.'

And then, even as she said the words, she knew they were untrue. In that very moment she knew one thing for an absolute certainty. She was in love with Caspar Reissman.

And she was in love with him in a way that made all her past experience fade into fantasy—what she felt now, with Caspar standing beside her in that cold spring wind, was both a delight and agony of an intensity she had never known before. He was her happiness: without him life was the pointless existence she had been enduring ever since she had left Florence—and even before that; her mistaken ideals had never made any real sense.

But with the joy of recognition came everything Monica had ever said about him—and what he had said about himself. He was not a man looking for serious commitment. And it seemed that, despite its shifting surface patterns, his relationship with Monica was probably the most stable he would ever tolerate. She could hear Monica's voice saying contemptuously, 'Married! That man doesn't even know the existence of the word!' Bianca was under no delusion that someone like Caspar would change his ideals for her. He was as physically attracted to her as she was to him, she was sure of that, but probably for him that was all it was. Whereas for her ... She had been blind not to have understood the nature of her feelings for him earlier—she must have fallen in love with him before she left Florence, but all her guilt and confusion over Hugh had prevented her from seeing it.

Yes. She knew now that she loved him. But it would be madness to tell him so. He already had too much power over her.

'Bianca?' He sounded hesitant—she had been silent for so long. Then she felt his hand cover hers on the cold stone of the parapet. His fingers were warm over her chilled ones, and she shivered involuntarily, as much at his touch as at the realisation of how cold she had grown.

As though he knew he had said enough, he took her hand in his, tucking it inside the flap of his pocket. 'Let's have a look in the Tower, shall we?'

She nodded without catching his eye.

They went to look at the Beefeaters after that, and into the armoury. The atmosphere between them, which had become dangerous with the undercurrents of which she was now silently aware, lightened a little, and she could almost forget the dark side to that moment of revelation by the river. She allowed herself to be carried along by his attempts to alter their mood, as they stood before a case full of medieval armour—Caspar was fascinated by the smallness of it.

'I don't suppose I could get into a single piece of that!' he commented incredulously.

She gave a half-smile, though she couldn't yet trust herself to catch his eye. 'That was made for a little dark Italian, not a six-foot blond Anglo-Goth!' she teased, and when he laughed and took her hand again, she didn't try to pull away.

Over lunch, in the small, discreetly expensive City restaurant where he had booked a table, they first talked about the Matisse—a safer subject than anything that touched on their own relationship.

'You're not about to lose your job,' he reassured her instantly. 'Antoniou's is blameless in the whole affair, unless some startling new evidence comes to light, which I doubt.'

'I thought it was all going to be so much more dramatic!' she exclaimed. 'Have they actually investigated Antoniou's? There hasn't been a whisper of it so far at the Gallery.'

'Geller must be aware of what's going on,' he replied, 'but the whole operation is being kept very low-key in order to catch the real villains. It isn't very exciting, and there's not much to add to what you already know. We guessed most of it in Florence.'

She smiled at him. '*You* guessed,' she said.

There was that familiar quirk to the corner of his mouth.

'Remember I told you about Jan van Heerlen? I visited his house in The Hague a couple of years ago with Johannes when he was copying the Matisse.'

'So that was when you "saw it being painted"—which I found it hard to believe?'

He smiled at her. 'Right—though I admit it did sound an unlikely claim at the time! Well, van Heerlen's house was stacked with valuable stuff, all of it inherited, but the police have discovered since that he has massive debts. He told Johannes that for sentimental reasons he wanted copies of the pictures he was going to have to sell . . . And the rest of the story is obvious.'

'Is it?' It didn't seem obvious to her, but then she was finding it difficult to think clearly, with him sitting opposite her at the table like that.

'Come on, Bianca—make an effort!' he teased. 'What did I tell you weeks ago was the probable explanation of the "forged" Matisse?'

'That van Heerlen was trying to make double the money by selling both the original, and the copy as the original original—if you see what I mean?'

Caspar laughed. 'That's a good way of putting it. He'd already sold a Cézanne twice over—one genuine, one copy—in two very private deals.'

'But how did he hope to get away with such a crazy scheme? He must have been mad to take such a risk!'

'Or very desperate. But, don't forget, everyone knew that he was the owner of the genuine paintings and had no reason to suspect him. He had a bit of luck with the Matisse. No one who knew anything about it, or who might have detected a copy, set eyes on it at any stage. Except me—by an extraordinary coincidence.'

'But why bother to send it to Antoniou's in the first place?' Bianca frowned. 'I'd have thought it'd be safer to keep it well away from any reputable dealers, and get it straight to the crooks. Pizzi is a crook?'

'He certainly is—and very cunning, which is why he's never been caught. The police have had their suspicions for some time, but they've never been able to prove anything. Because some unscrupulous people know he's a bit shady, and want access to things they wouldn't otherwise get, they use him. But I guess that the buyer of your Matisse wanted a guarantee that Pizzi wasn't cheating him, too. When a painting has been handled by a reputable gallery, it gives it some authentication, as you know. Van Heerlen took quite a risk with Antoniou's—which, as you assured me all along, is thoroughly respectable. But you have no top-flight experts there—and he was probably counting on the fact that Antoniou's hadn't any reason to suspect the painting in the first place.'

'And what about dealing with a shady customer like Pizzi?'

'Antoniou's have never used him before, and there was nothing wrong with the drawings—sketches towards a commission—that you were collecting.'

She gave a slow smile, looking him in the eyes. 'So do I get an apology for the way you treated me in Florence, and all your nasty accusations?'

'You're getting a good lunch—what more do you want?'

There was a hint of something more underlying the words, and he reached out and took her hand across the table, threading his fingers through hers. His touch, as always, melted her. She could hardly eat as it was, and had been toying with the food on her plate all the way through their conversation. It seemed that there was no way they could avoid the build-up of a highly charged atmosphere between them.

She made an attempt to defuse it. 'A written apology!' she demanded, with mock defiance.

He released her fingers, reaching in his inside jacket pocket to take out a gold-topped pen. There was a card advertising the special menu of the day on the table. He twitched it out of its holder, and wrote something across the back. She'd forgotten he was left-handed. Upside-down she recognised those beautiful flowing italics from the note he had once left for her in the apartment, but with his hand partially covering them she couldn't read what they said.

He held the little card out to her across the table, but he

didn't let her take it.

'Just one thing——' he said, his eyes holding hers. 'Your fiancé—have you fallen out of love with him, or he with you?'

'I told you we were never engaged . . .'

'And?'

'I think we've fallen out of love with each other,' she said quietly. Now he had forced her to admit it she knew that was the truth.

'So you've finished with him?'

'I told you earlier—I don't know. It's not easy to talk to Hugh about . . . us. He's never been keen on discussing things. And now I never really see him to try.'

Caspar didn't comment for a moment. Then he said slowly, 'It sounds as though you've got a major communication problem—has it always been like that?'

'We—we never needed to talk about serious things at the beginning. And then . . .' Bianca broke off. Should she be discussing any of this with the man she had fallen in love with, while there was still no clear sign that she had broken it off with Hugh? Caspar was a friend now, but it wasn't as simple as that. He wanted her, and given the chance he would take her if she let him. But she didn't dare let herself believe that there would be much more to it than the opportunism he confessed to—because if she persuaded herself there was love in it, and her fears turned out to be true, it would be far, far worse than what had happened with Hugh.

Caspar was watching her, almost as though he were trying to follow her thoughts in her face. He was still holding the card. Then he said slowly, 'I'm not just a disinterested observer, so I'm not sure I'm the one who should be saying this to you . . .'

He wasn't looking at her now, but at the card in his hand, and she doubted that he even saw it. He was flicking it absently with his thumbnail, almost unaware of what he was doing, fair eyebrows drawn together in a slight frown.

'Don't marry a man you can't communicate with—on every level . . . Kisses aren't enough—you have to be able to throw a few shoes too, like Monica.'

He looked up at her then, his eyes intense, as though he was trying to tell her something he wasn't prepared to put into words. And he was talking about communication? She had never seen him so hesitant. But what did he mean about not being disinterested—was he trying to tell her that he and Monica had the ideal relationship?

'How is Monica?' she asked carefully. And then wished she hadn't. His answer seemed to clear up for her the doubts she had just had.

'In residence.' He still wasn't looking at her, answering almost absently.

Her heart seemed to stop. 'You mean . . . she's moved back into your flat?'

'Monica's nothing if not persistent.'

'But I thought she'd fallen in love with someone called Marco—she was going to make you jealous!' she protested, trying not to give in to the sudden, terrifying jealousy that was racking her. But, of course, jealousy was a proof that there could still be love, and Monica had known that—she must be still in love with him, no matter what she said. Just as Bianca herself was in love with him—and they were both such fools . . . it hurt far too much to love someone like Caspar. He looked directly at her then, caught by something in her tone.

'Marco was another *bastardo*—like me. He lasted about two weeks, and then she decided she preferred the devil she knew.'

She didn't know what to say. What sort of a game was he playing between the two of them? He was as much of an enigma as ever. She wished she knew for certain he was sleeping with the Italian, then she could get angry with him for what he was trying to do to her, and maybe anger would hurt less than what she was feeling now.

'Where's your handbag?' he asked suddenly.

'What . . .?' The sudden switch of subject was confusing. 'Here—why?'

He took it from her and snapped it open, dropping the little white card inside, and then closing it again.

'You can read it when you get home.'

'Why?' she asked, astonished.

He met her eyes. 'Because I don't think you're in the right mood for it now . . . and anyway you're a hopeless actress—you'd have all the waiters hovering round you trying to get a look at it within seconds!'

She was so astounded that she laughed. He had taken her completely by surprise—shocking her out of the painful mood of doubt into curiosity. She never knew which direction he was going to take.

'I thought you were after my passport again!' she retaliated. What on earth had he written on the card, that he wouldn't let her see it?

The only thing she could be sure of after that was that she didn't want to say goodbye to Caspar yet. He was flying back the next day, and all the way back to the office she agonised with herself over whether she would ask him to supper with her.

Fulham was too dangerous—both her flatmates would be out for the evening, and although she desperately wanted to be alone with him she had a very good idea what would happen. It was stupid to encourage him—even if Monica had been out of the picture, there would still have been the whole question of his 'artist's freedom', which would never allow the kind of relationship she wanted.

They were on the Gallery doorstep before she'd decided what to do. 'Come and have supper at my mother's tonight?' she suggested, half wondering if he'd still be interested in seeing her. And then she added jokingly, 'She writes cookery books, so you can be sure of a good meal!' She didn't know what she'd do if he refused.

He looked down at her, smiling. 'And I was afraid you might have had enough of my company after some of the things I said . . . When we first met, you couldn't wait to get away from me—does this indicate a change of heart?'

It was safer to keep off the subject of her heart. And she couldn't pretend to understand what was going on in his—if he had one at all . . .

She gave him her mother's address in Richmond, and

stopped him from going up to the showrooms. If they appeared too friendly Mr Geller would never consent to sending her back to Florence at his persuasion. Caspar kissed her cheek as they stood in the narrow entrance to the Gallery staircase, and then was gone, striding off down the street. Almost as though this time *he* couldn't get away fast enough.

She had to switch to her 'Gallery manner' to deal with a customer almost as soon as she'd got to the top of the stairs, and, with both Alasdair and Frieda waiting impatiently for her return so that they could take their own lunchbreaks, she didn't have time to think of Caspar again until the end of a busy afternoon. She rang her mother to check that the dinner plans were convenient, but she knew that she could use the house even if Carla was out, and it would still be a better idea than Fulham. Her mother, adaptable as ever, didn't even comment when she told her it wasn't Hugh she was bringing.

When she was on her way to Richmond in the Tube, she suddenly remembered about Caspar's note. She managed to get it out of her bag with some difficulty in the rush-hour crowd, and tried to read it in such a way that the man standing next to her could get no clear view of it. One side harmlessly proclaimed '*Pâté en croûte* or *Champignons à la Grecque*', but when she flipped it over, the other was all too legible and bore no resemblance whatsoever to a respectable apology. She should have known . . !

> Darling Bianca,
> . . . let us prove,
> While we can, the sports of love . . .
> I'm sorry I said you weren't attractive when we first met. You are.
> Very. Come to bed?

Jolted against her neighbour by the movement of the train, she looked up from it at the same moment, and met his eyes—the speculation in them was blatant. She blushed to the roots of her hair, quickly crumpling the card in her hand and stuffing it into her coat pocket. Caspar had been right—she would never have been able to carry it off with sang-froid in the restaurant!

Although fitting her name to words from a famous poem must show that he had only meant it to startle her and amuse her in his usual way, she was sure the invitation was genuine—but it definitely suggested that it was the 'sports of love' he was after, rather than love itself. But even as a joke such an open declaration of it had its effect on her. The whole thing was outrageous, given the circumstances in which he had written it, but it was also disarming. Surely he couldn't be having a relationship with Monica if he could write that? But it wasn't very safe to rely on it . . .

It was in her mind all evening at her mother's, and she was on edge even before Caspar arrived—on time, which she wasn't expecting. He appeared very much in the 'City sophisticate's' mould at first, immaculately groomed as he had been earlier that day and so unlike the familiar painter that she hardly knew how to treat him. She wasn't sure how he'd hit it off with her mother—he looked like a variation on the Hugh theme—but from the warmth of her greeting to him it was clear that Carla had instantly taken to him. Before long he was in the kitchen discussing the photographs for her latest book with her, entirely at his ease.

Bianca herself actually felt a little intimidated by him at first. Also she was acutely conscious of the content of that note and guessed, from the way he looked at her, that Caspar knew she had read it. She was glad to let her mother take over the conversation—she hadn't felt so awkward in his company since they had first met, and she didn't begin to thaw out until, following her into the dining-room where she had gone to fetch some glasses, he caught her quickly round the waist from behind.

'I thought you liked men who dressed like bankers!' he teased. His voice in her ear made her shiver at his closeness. 'Well?' he demanded quietly. 'Was the apology "socially acceptable"?' It was a pointed reference to a conversation

they had had in Florence—when he had asked her if she
slept with Hugh.

'No,' she said, trying to extricate herself from the strong
arms that were pulling her closer.

'Why not?' His voice was low and seductive, and she felt
his lips against her neck. She knew she wouldn't be able
to resist him, but she didn't want to give in.

'Because of Monica!' she said, agonised. 'Caspar, don't!'

She began to struggle to get away from him, but he only
held her more tightly against him so that she could feel all
the masculine contours of that powerful frame the length
of her back.

'Monica has nothing to do with this,' he said. 'It's you I
want . . . Bianca, darling, please——'

Shuddering, she turned into his arms. She didn't wait to
find out what he was asking her, and she didn't really
care—one word had changed everything. It was only an
endearment, it didn't mean that he loved her, but it meant
more than Hugh had ever said to her in all the months of
their relationship. She had been fighting herself, as well as
him, and now she couldn't resist any longer. They were in
her mother's house—she was perfectly safe and nothing
could happen to her, except that the fires that were already
smouldering would be banked up even further against the
next time . . .

She opened her lips to his instantly, letting him explore
her mouth hungrily. Quickly, his hands slid down to her
hips, pulling her against him, and she tightened her arms
round his neck, pressing her breasts against the flat,
muscled wall of his chest. Desire blazed up in her,
unexpectedly strong, and she clung to him, melting flames
eating away at her inside. Had they been alone in the house,
she would have given herself to him without another
thought.

It was he who pulled away first. His heart was thundering
against hers, and he hid his face in her hair. They stood
like that for a while, but it did little to quiet the turmoil in
her own blood.

'I've wanted that for a long time,' he said at last. 'You

taste like honey.'

She gave an inarticulate little murmur, moving against him again, but he pushed himself away from her, holding her by the shoulders.

'Sweetheart, we've got to stop——' His voice was rough and unsteady. 'I won't be fit to talk to your mother. And it's not just my mind that's affected!'

There was a familiar gleam in the teasing blue eyes, but she knew what he meant. With his body so close against her own, she had known exactly what she was doing to him, and, caught up in that heady rush of passion, she hadn't cared about the consequences.

After that she felt slightly hysterical—it seemed impossible to reconcile the normal conversation that they had with her mother when they returned to the kitchen with those few intense, almost desperate moments she had just shared with Caspar.

Later, with a sense of relief, she left them talking. Caspar was much better than she at switching between two different worlds. As she set the dining-room table she thought about his comment on Monica—surely she was now safe in assuming that he really had no interest in resuming his former relationship?

When she rejoined them she found him sitting at the kitchen table with his jacket off, completely at home, drawing plans for a thorough reorganisation of his own domestic arrangements.

'If you like that colour,' her mother was saying, 'Bianca can take the paint out to you when she goes to Florence next. It has to be specially mixed.'

Bianca began to laugh, it seemed so unreal. 'Mamma, do you realise this man is one of the best-known British artists of his generation?' she demanded. 'That's what it said on our last catalogue, anyway. Don't you think he knows how to mix his own paint by now?'

'It's a difficult colour to match,' her mother replied, no whit abashed.

'You'd do better to reorganise his clothes,' Bianca said, with a sideways look at Caspar. Almost like a child, she wanted all his attention, and teasing him was one way to get it. He never failed to respond. 'His apartment's all right. It's just that he has no idea how to dress.'

Dark, petite, and immaculately attired herself, Carla eyed her guest critically. Why she had taken to him wasn't immediately obvious, but from the humour in her reply Bianca knew that her mother wholeheartedly approved of the unpredictable painter.

'Oh, I wouldn't say that—a bit Hugh-ish perhaps, but he looks remarkably well dressed to me.'

'I don't mean now—you should see him when he's in Florence! Horrible orange trousers and jerseys with paint all over them!'

Caspar gave her mother a long-suffering smile. 'Don't listen to her, Mrs James. When she turned up at my flat, she looked like something out of a Victorian orphanage—painted, of course, by D. G. Rossetti.'

'Rossetti never painted orphans!'

'You have a charming daughter, Mrs James,' he remarked with obvious irony.

Bianca, feeling slightly light-headed, saw her mother's glance go from her to Caspar and back again. Then she laughed; she had an infectious laugh, half husky, half squeaky. 'My name is Carla,' she said. It was the final accolade—even Hugh had never been asked to use her first name. She went on, 'I can see it wasn't Bianca's diplomatic way with words that won you over about the portrait!'

Caspar gave one of his quirky sideways smiles, but he was looking at Bianca. 'No,' he said slowly. 'Not exactly. But she has her methods . . .'

CHAPTER EIGHT

FLORENCE—at last they were sending her back there! The three weeks since Caspar had left seemed an eternity.

'You're to deliver some photographs and provenance reports to Cavalli's,' Joseph Geller instructed her. 'We're not dealing with Giacomo Pizzi any more.' She thought he gave her an odd look at that point, and decided that there must have been more going on behind the scenes than she had been aware of. She wondered if Geller could have heard something about Monica, and the fact that she'd let the so-called Matisse out of her hands. Fake or no fake, she should never have let anyone else deliver it, though in the circumstances she wasn't sure what else she could have done.

She didn't say anything. No one had breathed a word of a forgery at the Gallery, and that was probably the way it was going to stay—especially if they were all in the clear, as Caspar had said. It wouldn't do Antoniou's any good if word got about that they'd let a forgery slip through their hands.

'You're to bring back the portrait of Mrs Brandt, which is now ready, I understand. Caspar Reissman asked for you particularly—I gather he made some studies of you for a portrait, and he wants to finish it.'

She gaped at him, and was about to deny it when she had second thoughts. Perhaps Caspar had made up this story to persuade the Gallery to send her back. There couldn't be much truth in it—he hadn't made any sketches of her.

'Yes,' she agreed cautiously, and then truth compelled her to admit, 'But I didn't actually sit for him.'

'I heard he took you out to lunch when he was here a few weeks ago?' Was she imagining it, or was there almost a twinkle behind the spectacles?

Afterwards, as she tried not to skip out round his office door, she decided it must have been her imagination—the rest of his face was as dry and disapproving as ever.

She was longing to see Caspar. Apart from those few moments alone together in her mother's house, they had never really expressed any of the mutual attraction that had now built to such an intensity between them. Their parting had been almost casual in comparison, as though both were frightened of being betrayed into that overwhelming need for each other again. It had happened so suddenly.

She knew that whatever it was between them now had to be worked out in Florence. From her point of view she was free at last to explore her relationship with him in any way she chose. There was no Hugh any longer; she was glad they had had one last scene, which she, of course, had provoked, and which had proved something of a revelation about her perfect Englishman.

Since that moment by the Thames in the cold spring wind when she had discovered she loved Caspar, she had been haunted by the thought that although her relationship with Hugh had appeared to be falling apart, he might not have seen it like that. She knew she could no longer continue with it, but it was only honest to tell him so. There must be a definite end.

It was about a week after Caspar had gone, a Friday evening. She took the car to work, and decided to drive back to Richmond via Sloane Square and call in, on the off-chance of seeing Hugh.

She felt nervous about facing him once she got to the flats, and wondered if she was really doing the right thing as she pressed the bell opposite his name-plate. It didn't seem tactful to use her key.

'Hello?' Hugh's voice sounded over the intercom.

'Hugh—it's me, Bianca. Can I come up?'

There was a second's hesitation before he spoke, and her heart sank. 'OK. The door's open.'

There was an electronic buzz, and the door swung open under her hand.

She knew the answer to everything she had come to find out the minute Hugh opened the door of his flat to her. There was nothing she could put her finger on; just something about his manner that told her. There's someone else here, she thought. Someone he doesn't want me to meet.

'Bianca! What a surprise. Are you on your way home from work?' Of course she was. He knew that very well. He made no move to kiss her until she reached up to give him a peck on the cheek.

'I thought I'd call in. We haven't seen each other for such a long time. Not since the Southcotts' drinks party.'

'No. Well. As I told you, things have been a bit busy.' Was she imagining it, or did he look embarrassed?

'Can I come in and have a drink?'

They were still standing in the elegantly decorated hallway with its chandelier and spindly-legged antiques. In the old days he'd have taken her coat off for her, and told her to help herself to whatever she wanted—and to pour him a drink, too.

He seemed to come to a decision. 'Of course. Come in. I've got someone here . . .'

She had known it.

'I think you know Charlotte Wakeham, Simon's secretary, don't you? Charlotte, this is Bianca.'

Charlotte smiled a charming social smile, and said, 'Of course—we've met.'

And after that nothing was said but a lot of social chitchat that wasn't very interesting, but told Bianca one thing very clearly: Charlotte was completely at her ease, as though she had every right to be there, and that spoke volumes about her relationship with Hugh. She didn't call him 'darling', or make any remark that wasn't also addressed to Bianca, but her eyes caught his once or twice in a way that showed that there was already some sort of understanding between them.

Bianca left as soon as she decently could. Hugh got up to see her to the door. He looked relieved.

What did he expect me to do? she wondered. Throw an

Italian fit and hurl my drink at Charlotte—or cry and make a terrible scene? It *was* hurtful to think that he was prepared to evade the truth like that—that he hadn't had the courage to tell her he was seeing another woman when all the time he was supposed to be in love with her. If things had been different, perhaps she would have cried, or made it much more awkward for him. She didn't feel very pleased with herself, even though she was far more honest than he had been.

'Bye, Bianca—thanks for dropping in. It was good to see you.' He sounded genuine.

He actually kissed her cheek without having to be prompted. Yes, she thought, I bet it is good to see me now that I've done all the unpleasant bit for you!

'Goodbye, Hugh——' Then she couldn't resist a parting shot—her Italian pride demanded it, if nothing else!

She held out her keys to him—his keys—and dropped them into his hand. 'Don't worry—I won't be calling round uninvited again! *We* never used to like uninvited callers much, did we?' Her eyes, an astonishing amber yellow, blazed for a second into his grey ones. Yes, she thought again. You coward!

Almost as though he had read the thought quite clearly, he blinked, looking a little startled. Then she turned on her heel and fled down the stairs to the street. She couldn't get away soon enough.

Well-mannered, well-dressed, efficient, *boring* Charlotte! she thought all the way home to her mother's. But, of course, she was Hugh's ideal—the stereotype of the perfect English upper-middle-class wife. I don't suppose I'd ever have turned myself into a very convincing version of that, she told herself. I should be pleased I didn't make a terrible mistake in marrying him . . . But then, he'd never proposed.

She wasn't pleased about what had happened, but she wasn't exactly sad, either—just empty. One whole part of her life had come at last to an end, and what was she left with? A new love that for all sorts of reasons looked as though it was going to prove much more of a disaster than the old . . . The man didn't even live in the same country, for a start—and he certainly didn't share her ideals about marriage . . .

But unexpectedly, if she had had any doubts about how she should feel over what had happened with Hugh, her mother would have quickly dispelled them.

'You're very silent tonight,' she remarked later that evening.

'It's Hugh . . .' Bianca admitted quietly. 'He's going to marry someone else, and I'm not quite sure I've got used to the idea yet.'

'Well, I'm delighted!' Carla James exclaimed heartily. 'He was totally wrong for you.'

'But, Mamma—'

Trial recipe in hand, Carla pushed her spectacles down on her nose and surveyed her daughter critically.

'But Mamma nothing!' she said firmly. 'He was totally wrong for you, my love. A nice young man in his way, but a bit too ambitious, and far too well-mannered in every situation for my liking. I began to wonder if there were any real feelings there at all—and he was trying to turn you into a machine. When you were with him I scarcely recognised my lively, impulsive, fun-loving daughter. You were too scared of putting a foot wrong. That's no basis for a good relationship.'

'But I thought you liked him!'

'I did. I do,' said her mother huskily. 'But that doesn't make him the right person for you to marry.'

'Why didn't you say all this before?' Bianca asked, half annoyed by her mother's response.

'Would it have made any difference if I had?' She slipped a comforting arm round her daughter's shoulders. 'So your heart is broken?'

Bianca gave her a rueful grin. 'You always say there's no such thing as a broken heart . . . and anyway . . . I . . . it's . . .' She didn't know how to go on. After months of mooning over Hugh it would sound so fickle.

'There's someone else?' her mother prompted gently.

'Oh, Mamma, I'm so confused!'

Her mother was silent for a moment. 'I don't suppose

that confusion would have anything to do with a certain
portrait painter you brought home to supper recently,
would it?' she asked carefully.

'No, of course not!' she denied, a little too quickly to be
convincing, and then, catching her mother's sceptical eye,
admitted, 'Well, yes ... but he's just a no-good opportunist,
and all he wants to do is sleep with me. He doesn't want
to get married. He thinks artists should be completely
free——' She could feel herself getting hopelessly worked
up even talking about it. 'I don't even know if he's still living
with his other girlfriend, and when I ask him he just says
that she has nothing to do with *us*—which could mean
anything—and I'm not going to be *anyone's* mistress! I think
I'll give up men forever!'

Carla James, long accustomed to her daughter's
outbursts, didn't turn a hair at the emotional confession.

'Good,' she approved calmly. 'Now perhaps you could
devote yourself to the broccoli. It'll be green mush if you
leave it any longer.'

Everything Bianca had said to her mother about Caspar
was true, but it didn't stop her indulging in dangerous
dreams on the way to Florence. She smiled to herself when
she remembered the way his tow-coloured hair stuck out
when he ran his hand through it, and that blue sparkle his
eyes always had when he was amused, and that long
lizard's mouth! It was odd how used she'd got to the image
of him as he had been in Italy—untidy, paint-smeared,
smelling of linseed oil. The London image had been just
as true to him in some ways as that of the down-at-heel
painter, but well-dressed, conventionally handsome men
no longer appealed to her. Hugh had cured her of that.

There was no doubt that Caspar could play the part of
a Hugh if he chose: he had as much calculation, and steel,
under that careless exterior. But Hugh could never be a
Caspar. Now, in comparison with the painter, she could
see his limitations. He lacked real humour, and
spontaneity, and passion—and he inhibited them in her.
Caspar had all those things. And there was a spirit of

generosity about him—it came to her now with a sense of shock that she would never have described Hugh as a generous man. He was too self-centred.

She no longer felt any disloyalty in comparing them. Caspar had shown her what was lacking from her former relationship, and now that that was ended she was free to find out just how much he meant to her. But, with no guilt over Hugh to hold her back from a commitment that might ultimately prove destructive to her, only her own sense of self-preservation could keep her from becoming fully involved with Caspar. She suspected that it would be a very fragile barrier where love was concerned.

Ever since seeing Caspar in London she had been frightened by the power of her own feelings—she had never suspected that she could feel such jealousy over another woman, or such hunger for a man, and she knew that, if he made a serious attempt to seduce her, there was no way she was going to be able to resist him.

She would have to be very, very careful never to see him alone.

It was late afternoon by the time she had reached Florence. She had spoken to Caspar very briefly on the phone the night before, and he had told her to look out for him at the railway station—there was just a chance he might be able to meet her. But with the inevitable delays after an alteration in her flight time, she wasn't surprised that there was no sign of him when the train pulled in. It didn't stop her being unreasonably disappointed, though.

She took a taxi to her hotel—near the Piazza della Republica, as before—and tried to phone him as soon as she arrived. She listened to the ringing tone in such a state that she hardly knew what she was going to say, but there was no answer.

She tried at half-hourly intervals after that, but time passed, and she began to feel increasingly anxious. It was too late to take the photographs and the rest to Cavalli's now. Where *was* Caspar?

It was he who rang her in the end, after seven.

'Bianca? I'm sorry—I hoped to see you hours ago. I called

the airport, and they said your flight was delayed. Can you meet me?' His voice sounded warm and friendly, but as though half his mind was on something else.

'Yes, of course!' She felt absurdly relieved to hear him. 'Where are you phoning from? There's an awful lot of noise in the background.'

'I'm in the café I took you to, near the Ponte Vecchio—where we had lunch and you met Stephen—do you remember it? Listen, sweetheart . . .'

'Wh-what?' A delicious dizzy sensation flooded right through her. One word, as before, could change her entire world. She was not merely 'in love' with him—she was hopelessly, desperately in love—all her cautious resolutions on the plane meant nothing to her now! She didn't care what happened as long as there was some way she could tell him—show him—how much he meant to her.

'Bianca, are you listening?'

'What? Yes, yes, I am . . .'

'For the third time—weren't you supposed to be delivering something to Cavalli's?'

'Yes . . . how did you know?' It was difficult to concentrate on what he was actually saying. All that mattered was the sound of his voice.

'Geller told me he'd find you something else to do when he was negotiating about Mrs B.—probably wanted to make the most of the air ticket. Have you been round there yet?'

'These things aren't frauds, surely?' she asked, trying to pull her thoughts together and only half in jest.

She heard him laugh again—that wonderful, familiar shout of laughter she remembered from their first crazy meeting.

'Not as far as I know! You don't have to deliver them tonight, do you? Where are they now? I want you round here for a very special reason.'

'Here, in the hotel safe . . . Caspar.'

'What?'

There was a long pause while she wondered what she could say—she wanted to tell him so much! 'It doesn't matter,' she said at last. 'Nothing.'

'See you as soon as you can get here!' he said. 'I'm celebrating something.' And then he hung up.

All the way to the Arno her happiness made her so light-headed she felt she could fly. She *would* be careful—she would! She only wanted to see him . . . and they were meeting in a café, in a crowd of people—there wasn't anything dangerous about that . . . She noticed nothing as she sped towards the Ponte Vecchio—the old streets, the shops, the pedestrians were just a meaningless blur. She had to stop herself sprinting twice.

The café was easy to find; she remembered the street, just off a little piazza with a fountain in it. The last vestiges of caution prompted her to stand back from the doorway, a little out of sight of the window, when she arrived flushed and breathless, her eyes like stars. The last thing she wanted to give away was just how much she felt for him—he would instantly take advantage of it, and she couldn't afford that. She was far too vulnerable.

She raked her fingers through her hair, pushing it back from her face, and tried to breathe evenly. Then she stepped into the doorway, and went in.

The first thing that really hit her was the noise, and then the warmth of the atmosphere in contrast with the cold spring evening outside. There was a lot of talk and laughter against the background of piped music, and what looked like crowds of people grouped round some tables that were pushed together in the middle. What had Caspar said—a celebration or something? She recognised Caspar's friend Stephen in the crowd of faces nearest her, but then, as the grouping pattern round the tables shifted, her eyes were drawn to two people sitting in the centre. They were facing her—the woman with red hair laughing, sitting in the lap of the man who had his arms round her. One of her hands was in his hair, and the other stroked his cheek . . . And from then on each detail branded itself upon her vision with distinct and painful clarity.

The man was also laughing, then suddenly he pulled the woman closer and kissed her. It was a prolonged, intimate kiss, and to the stunned Bianca it seemed to go on forever. It was almost as though she were compelled to watch in some sort of horrible trance, every separate part of a second an agony all of its own. Suspended in a dreadful clamorous silence, aware of a rushing in her ears and the thunder of her own heartbeats, she wondered vaguely if she was going to faint.

Then the rushing noise cleared, and the shouting, clapping and cheering broke in on her as the couple brought their long embrace to an end, and the man looked up. Teasing blue eyes met hers, and at that instant Bianca felt as though someone had just hit her with a sledgehammer of ice.

Monica and Caspar . . . of course. Now it seemed so obvious. What a naïve fool she'd been. He'd even told her Monica was back in his flat—he'd given her no clear answer when she'd asked about her . . .

'Bianca!'

At the very moment she had gathered her wits to escape, Stephen had recognised her. His greeting turned other heads—all of them strangers—and then Monica, still in Caspar's lap, waved.

'Bianca *cara*! Come here and congratulate me—I'm engaged!'

Someone said in Italian, 'She's got him at last!' and laughed.

Then all the other sounds that had been blocked from her mind before became suddenly clear—every word, laugh, scrape of a chair, chink of a glass. And she could not tear her eyes from Caspar—Caspar with his arms round Monica.

He was laughing still, then flung out one arm carelessly towards Bianca herself. He called to her, 'Bianca—come and join us! Monica is just showing me how much she still loves me!'

Her own love was over before it had begun. It was Monica he really cared for; all the signs had been there—she had seen them, but she hadn't wanted to believe them. And they had been together for years. She couldn't blame the Italian—she had wanted Caspar all along. What did Bianca herself matter to him? An amusement, that was all, when things weren't going well with his real mistress. She'd allowed herself to be seduced by that flattering charm, persuading herself that a shared sexual attraction must also mean that his feelings were in some way involved. But she should have gone by her first impressions of him—an opportunist with no real feelings at all. Even his rows had been acting.

He mustn't find out what I feel—he mustn't, she told herself desperately.

Her face set, she found herself being pushed towards him. Then mechanically she was kissing Monica on both cheeks, accepting a wine glass from someone, and Caspar was leaning back behind the woman in his lap, pulling her towards him with one arm.

'Bianca!' he said again. 'We've been waiting for you—'

He reached up and tugged her long hair, forcing her to bend to him, and then kissed her. She turned her face just in time so that his lips touched the side of her cheek.

He pulled still tighter, winding his fingers in the wavy curls so that his mouth was close to her ear.

'What's the matter?' His voice was so low that she doubted what he said was audible even to Monica.

She tried to smile brightly. 'Nothing! Except you're hurting me . . .' In a way you'll never know, she added silently. She blinked quickly. He could attribute her swimming eyes to the way he had just pulled her hair.

She turned away as he released her, coming face to face with Stephen, who'd followed in her wake.

'Got any more forgeries with you this time? Caspar told me about the Matisse—Pizzi and his crew have been the talk of Florence ever since. Most of them will be behind bars by the end of the year!' Stephen was smiling at her, keen to chat, and out of the corner of her eye she was aware that Caspar's attention was being claimed by someone else.

She made conversation automatically; the months she'd spent trying to be the ideal employee at Antoniou's had enabled her to do that. They talked art, and forgeries, and what he was painting, and her mind was on none of it. All she could think of was Caspar and Monica—sitting somewhere behind her now as she took every opportunity to edge herself nearer and nearer to the far side of the restaurant, and escape.

Someone else joined in the conversation. He was introduced, and she didn't even listen to his name. There were still so many people between her and the door . . .

She was forced to turn a little, glimpsing as she did so Monica, in the arms now of a tall, swarthy Italian, dancing to the taped music. Then strong arms slipped round her own waist from behind, and a familiar cheek brushed against hers.

'Come and dance with me for a while—it's too early to leave yet.'

She went rigid, her spine bristling with awareness of him. She could feel his body, lean and so unexpectedly athletic, pressed against hers, and for one traitorous instant she was almost overwhelmed by the desire to turn into his arms, and let him do whatever he wanted with her.

His lips touched her neck. 'What's wrong, sweetheart?'

Sweetheart . . . oh, what a fool she'd been when such endearments came so easily to him! He should be keeping them for Monica; or was he such a free-living artist that he was telling her that fidelity in marriage wouldn't mean much to him—he would still be in the market for other women?

Frantically, she tried to prise his arms away from her.

'Stop it, Caspar! Hadn't you better keep this sort of thing for Monica? It doesn't amuse *me*.'

Anger, a fiery screen to hide the hurt inside her, flared up. How could he—how dared he play with her like this! Did he think that women had no feelings worth considering, that he could switch from one to another as though they were mechanical dolls designed purely for his amusement? Monica had called him a bastard—she was right. And if she was fool enough to marry him, she deserved him!

With sudden unexpected force Bianca broke from him,

and pushed her way to the door, scarcely aware of anyone in her path, or of the burly Italian trying to enter the café. He blocked the exit momentarily, but she pushed round him into the street. He must have got in Caspar's way too, if he had tried to follow her. She didn't know.

She ran to the nearest side turning and darted down it, branching off again at random at the nearest junction. No one was following her.

She slowed to a halt. Of course he wouldn't follow her. He was engaged to someone else—the man who believed in complete freedom for the artist. She meant nothing serious to him—she never had. All those things she had wanted to interpret as signs that he might be falling in love with her meant nothing more than that he wanted her in bed.

But perhaps underneath she had known that all along. The word *love* had never once been mentioned between them. She was a fool to let herself indulge in the sort of dreams that could only end in pieces. She had been deluding herself that she would be careful, that she wouldn't commit herself too far . . . it had long been too late as far as her heart was concerned. Now she knew for certain that she was nothing but a kind of interlude for him—he had wanted her in London, but he wanted Monica when he was in Florence, where his life was. The real game was with Monica.

She started to walk again, aware that she might draw unwelcome attention to herself if she didn't appear to have some purpose. She was in the maze of back-streets that ran off the Via Guicciardini and although she took turnings at random, she knew she couldn't get lost. She was never far from the river.

The high façades of the buildings crowded in on her; the alleys were not well lit, and it was already dusk. Washing, unnaturally white in the gloom, was strung from side to side above her head between the high windows with their wooden shutters pinned back against the peeling, stuccoed walls. Her eye registered the details, while her mind followed its own unhappy paths.

It was fully dark by the time she crossed the Arno and made for her hotel. Telling herself that nothing had really changed—that she could still deliver the photographs and papers to Cavalli's in the morning, and that she would only have to see Caspar briefly to collect the portrait—didn't make any difference to the knowledge that she had fallen in love with the wrong man. A man whose interests were already committed elsewhere, only she had been too blind to see it, wanting to interpret the histrionics of his relationship with Monica as a sign that he didn't really care for her.

She told herself she still had her independent life in London if she wanted it, and her job. And getting a famous portrait painter to change his work against his better judgement had definitely enhanced her status at work, now that Mr Geller had got over it. But none of this was any real consolation, and just at the moment she hated the very existence of the portrait: if it hadn't been for Mrs Brandt, she would never have met Caspar Reissman.

Exhausted and miserable, she found herself in the entrance to the hotel foyer. She had no idea what time it was. Perhaps she should have a bath and go to bed. She hadn't eaten anything, but she felt more sick than hungry. First she would ask Reception to contact the airport for her—she would book a flight for tomorrow evening. Florence had no appeal for her any longer . . .

He was waiting for her. The tall figure rose from one of the deep armchairs as she crossed to the reception desk. His hair was untidy, in a way that suggested he'd run his hands through it too often; the cuffs of his jacket and his shirtsleeves were pushed up carelessly on the strong forearms with their dusting of gold hair, and he glanced at the heavy gold watch on his wrist as she caught sight of him.

His mouth was grim and his eyes . . . blue as arctic ice. 'Bianca,' he said. In his voice was an edge of anger barely under control. 'Where the *hell* have you been?'

CHAPTER NINE

BIANCA stared at Caspar, too astonished to say anything. What was he doing here? He should be with Monica. When she did try to speak, her voice seemed to catch in her throat.

'What I do is no concern of yours!' It was a childish reply, but she didn't want to see him now—she couldn't cope with any of it.

'It *is* my concern—you were supposed to be meeting me at that café. I've been searching half Florence for you. What made you walk out like that?' He sounded coldly furious, as though she'd deliberately insulted him.

What was he doing here? What right had he to come and demand explanations of her? Tired as she was, his temper was sparking hers.

'You obviously had other things on your mind!' she accused angrily. 'What was I supposed to do—hang round waiting for a few words every time you and Monica took a break?'

'Bianca—'

But she wasn't staying to listen to whatever feeble explanations he was going to think up.

'I feel very sorry for her!' Fatigue would make her hysterical if she wasn't careful, and now she'd started it was difficult to stop. 'I suppose this is the way you're going to go on after you're married . . . you shouldn't even be here, and I bet she doesn't know where you are! I'm tired and I want to go to bed—if you've got something to say about the portrait, you can ring me tomorrow. I don't want to discuss *anything* with you now!'

She turned on her heel, hair flying, to head for the reception desk and her room key, but before she could take a step he had caught her by the arm, his fingers digging into the soft flesh above the elbow.

'But there's plenty *I* want to discuss with you! And the only choice you get is where it happens—my apartment or here.'

'You can't dictate to me!' she flashed at him. 'I'm not having any of your so-called discussions in the middle of a hotel reception area, or shut up with you in your flat!'

'Then we'll talk in the street.' For a moment his eyes held hers—cold steel compelling her gaze. No wonder Monica threw things at him. It was one way of defusing some of that dangerous aggression she could sense in him, simmering below the surface.

She thought of defying him, then instantly abandoned the idea. She wouldn't get the better of him, and it would only make an embarrassing public scene—something she minded about more than Monica did, and certainly more than he did.

He must have read capitulation in her eyes, because he got her out in the street so fast she wasn't sure how it happened.

Then they were walking quickly towards the river, neither willing to break the tense and angry silence. In a less hostile mood she might have cried. It was the beginning of April in Florence; there were lights from the bridges reflected in the river, and lovers wandering hand in hand about the darkened streets. The contrast was almost too much to bear. Everything that could have been romance had melted away in a few hours.

The fact that he was going to marry Monica made no difference to what she felt for him. It just made it the more painful that he should be seeking her out now.

Bianca scarcely noticed where they were going. They crossed a bridge somewhere, but she had no idea which one, nor of the direction in which they were walking. Their silent antagonism stretched like a barbed-wire fence along the ___ ment between them.

___ hey came upon a deserted square, and an old ___ ain, long dry, in the middle of it. Their angry ___ lowed, and they were somewhere in the ___ old artisans' quarter where Caspar had his apartment. It was dark now, and light poured out from a workshop doorway, where a couple of carpenters were still working elaborately carved picture frames. Drawn by the glow, she slowed to a halt, gazing in unseeing, her thoughts full of the hateful silence between herself and Caspar. Abruptly he took hold of her arm, pulling her to one side, and backed her against a wall out of sight of the workshop. Then he put a hand either side of her, leaning his weight a little towards her, trapping her.

'Bianca, look at me!' His eyes, glittering in the half dark, searched hers. '*Say* something—I can't bear this!'

'What do you want me to say?' she asked, her voice spiked with suppressed emotion. He was too close; every inch of her body was reacting to him.

He made a small, impatient sound. 'What the hell's the matter with you? You weren't like this in London. Is it Hugh, or me, or what?'

She stared at him. What *could* she say? Why did you have to make me fall in love with you when it's all so pointless? Some of it added up, more or less, to make a kind of sense. He had said they were friends. But he had also called himself an opportunist, and he had said he wanted to go to bed with her, which must mean that sex had little significance for him beyond the immediate pleasure.

What didn't make sense was the complication of Monica ... What happened to friendship when he wanted both of them? Or did he really not know the effect he was having on Bianca herself?

But even if there were no Monica, it wouldn't be any good. It would just be what had happened with Hugh all over again—only it would be much, much worse this time.

'Why didn't you tell me before that you were engaged to Monica?' she demanded miserably.

'Because——' And then he stopped, his eyes assessing her, as though he was trying to read everything she was so anxious to hide. 'Why should that make any difference?' he asked, his voice quieter now.

She couldn't tell him the truth; and she couldn't think

of an answer.

'OK,' he went on suddenly. 'So what if I am engaged to her? Why should you be upset about it? I thought you and she got on like a house on fire. Didn't you devise some little mutual aid scheme last time you were here?'

'It's because I do like her!' she said fiercely. 'I feel sorry for her for being stupid enough to marry a bastard like you! I suppose you find it amusing to play around with two women at once! And in the future—is your idea of marriage leaving one woman at home while you chase another round Florence in the dark whenever you feel a bit bored?' Now she had started, it was difficult to stop. 'What are you doing with me, when you've only just got engaged to her? Maybe you think she doesn't mind—but I assure you she does! And I mind—I mind a lot. Just leave me alone and go back to her, will you? I've had more than I can take of this.'

To her surprise his anger had vanished. He was looking at her quite differently now. Then, 'You're jealous,' he said softly. 'Wonderfully, spectacularly jealous.'

She stared at him in resentment—so what if she was? He was the one behaving unacceptably, not she.

'I've never played around with two women in my life!' He wasn't taking her seriously. The amused gleam in his eye told her that.

'You know perfectly well what I mean!'

'And you are upset on Monica's account?'

'Yes!'

'But that's not the whole of the story, is it?'

She was silent.

'Bianca,' he said gently, 'come back to the apartment with me.'

He was too clever for her; she couldn't keep hold of her anger. Against her will she found it ebbing away, and with it most of her strength to resist him. She had promised herself she wouldn't be alone with him, but the mere fact of his physical closeness weakened all her defences. She hesitated.

'It's all right——' he reassured her, as though reading her

thoughts '—there's someone there I want you to meet.'

She didn't think too clearly about that. Maybe it was Monica who was there—maybe seeing them together once more would cure her of longing for the impossible.

When she didn't reply he took her hand, lacing his long artist's fingers through hers. His thumb caressed her wrist. He was standing so close to her she couldn't any longer ignore her awareness of him—her whole body was shrieking their physical contact.

'Yes?' he asked.

Again she didn't answer, still hesitating on the edge of a decision that could be the most stupid one of her entire life. Involuntarily her hand tightened in his grasp, and at the same time a voice in her head warned, Be careful! But she had already given in. She looked up at him. His eyes, unreadable, considered her.

'Monica apart, are you pleased to see me?' he asked quietly.

'Monica apart . . . yes. I am.'

'And Hugh?'

She looked down, concentrating on the open collar of his shirt, unwilling to let him read any of her feelings too clearly. 'Hugh is in love with somebody else. It's finished.'

'Then . . . hello, Bianca.'

'Hello, Caspar.'

She was leaning against the wall, her feet between his. She didn't move as he bent towards her. His lips touched hers very gently—and that was all. There was still Monica.

The question was harder to ask than she had thought—but, after all, what could he say that she didn't know already?

'Caspar——'

'What?'

'If you're engaged to Monica, what are you doing with me?'

He put two fingers under her chin, forcing her to lift her head so she could look him directly in the eyes.

'If I'm engaged to Monica, what are *you* doing with *me*?'

Then something occurred to her. 'Who is it at the

apartment—is it Monica?' she asked suddenly. Surely she wouldn't have let him out of her sight the night of their engagement party?

'No . . . she's probably out with her fiancé by now.'

She stared at him, unable to take in for a moment the implications of what he had said.

'What?' Her voice was scarcely above a whisper.

'It was you who told me I was engaged to Monica.'

He wasn't going to marry Monica . . . he wasn't——! The relief that surged through her almost instantly gave way to further confusion. There was something that didn't make sense in all this: he had realised long before she had the mistake she had made . . . so why hadn't he told her?

'But—but in the café—and just now! You knew what I thought! Why didn't you say something?'

He traced a line down the side of her face with one finger, his expression serious, but he evaded her question. 'Come back to the apartment and meet someone.'

'How do I know they'll be there?—I don't want to be alone with you!'

'Why not?'

'Because I don't trust you.'

His eyes again assessed her thoughtfully. 'There's something behind that remark that you're not telling me, but until you'll admit it we're not going to make any progress. So if I promise you you won't be alone—our visitor should have arrived by now—will you come?'

She desperately wanted his company—and now the thought of returning alone to the hotel was unbearable. Maybe it was courting disaster to agree to spend more time with him, but there was still too much uncertain. Perhaps she should trust him for once.

'All right,' she said at last.

He gave her then the sort of smile that made her heart turn over, and she smiled back, a little warily still, thinking all the while how strange it was that when they'd first met none of his smiles, angelic or otherwise, had had the slightest effect on her.

They walked through the dark old streets in a different

kind of silence this time. With Caspar's hand in hers, she could have wandered indefinitely like that. This way it was easy; uncomplicated. He was her companion, and friend, and she was free to go on loving him in a way that involved no rejections.

She saw now how she had jumped to the wrong conclusions about him—jealousy had caused her to misinterpret what she'd witnessed in the café. She should have recognised that kiss for what it was: yet another example of the exaggerated behaviour that typified his relationship with his one-time mistress, and no more than that. They understood each other. But he had told her the truth when he had said, a long time ago, that he had no interest in resuming their former relationship.

The apartment was in darkness. Caspar switched on a light as they entered.

'I thought you said you were expecting a visitor,' she said carefully. Please, Caspar, she prayed silently, don't start now. I can't take any more tonight.

'I was—I am,' he said, switching on more lights. 'He can't be relied on to be punctual, but he'll turn up eventually. Never one to miss a free drink.'

'Who is it?' She wasn't really interested. She didn't know whether she could believe him or not.

'Someone who's very keen to meet you.'

'Why?' She felt so tired. The emotion of the last few hours seemed to have drained everything out of her. She looked round for somewhere to sit down. The apartment was actually tidy, and there were several chairs round the dining table. Now that she was engaged to someone else, Monica no longer needed them for bargaining purposes.

'He's . . . heard about you,' he said non-committally. 'Take your jacket off—you look as though you're about to leave any minute.'

'Perhaps I am,' she said quietly. 'You told me we wouldn't be alone.'

He came to stand behind her and, ignoring her implied protest, began to strip off the light jacket she wore. She did nothing to resist him—a physical fight was the last thing she wanted.

'We won't be.' He tossed the jacket on to the sofa, and slipped his arms round her, kissing her ear. 'Don't be so tense, my sweet. What do you think is going to happen to you?'

She tried to pull away from him. 'Don't, Caspar!'

'Then tell me why you were so upset about Monica.'

'I told you . . . because I like her, and I thought you were messing around with both of us——'

He didn't wait for her to finish. 'But that's not all of it, is it? If you were only upset about Monica, you wouldn't still be so uptight with me—and you are, aren't you?'

He turned her round to face him, and she tried to step back out of his grasp, but he was holding her firmly by the shoulders. 'You weren't like this when we were in London.' He wasn't going to let her escape.

How ironic. This was a reverse of what had happened with Hugh—this time it was she who was so unwilling to talk.

'What's happened since then?' he pursued. 'Is it because you've broken up with Hugh? Or is it because you were jealous of Monica when you thought she was going to marry me, and you walked out of the bar when you saw me kissing her—you didn't like it when you thought the kisses I gave her were better than the kisses I give you?'

'I'm *not* jealous!' she denied vehemently.

'No, you're not jealous now—you're angry about something, I can see it in your eyes. But you were. Come on, Bianca—admit it.'

To admit to jealousy was to admit to love. She couldn't bear it any longer—he just seemed to be playing with her.

'*Don't*, Caspar! I can't talk now—I don't want to! And I don't believe in this friend of yours, either—I want to go!' She struggled to free herself, trying to twist out of his grasp.

'Let me go!' She was almost shouting at him now, in the panic that had begun to rise in her. She couldn't stay here any longer—she wasn't sure if she believed in his visitor or not, but one thing she was certain of was that he would take advantage of the fact that they were alone. As always, they sparked each other. She caught a dangerous flash in his eyes.

'Why won't you trust me? Do you think I've lied to you deliberately? You've got a bloody low opinion of me, haven't you! What do you think I want to do, for heaven's sake? Rape you? Why can't you be honest with me—or has all that business about Monica's *bastardo* got to you so that you can't see the truth? Bianca, *look* at me when I'm talking to you!'

'You've got no right to ask me anything!' she shouted. 'You deliberately didn't tell me the truth about you and Monica—just so you could play some twisted little game! I suppose you find it amusing to see me upset!'

'Keep your voice down—do you want the whole piazza to hear?'

'They should be used to it by now with the sort of life you lead!' She didn't care what she said. She'd never known that she could feel so angry.

'It didn't matter before, but with you it does!' he said fiercely. 'Bianca, will you *stop*!' He shook her, hurting her till she gasped.

'Let go of me!' Almost hysterical, she broke from him as his hold relaxed. Her jacket was on the sofa, but she snatched up the first thing that came to her hand—and she threw it at him. The cushion missed by yards, but then she found herself clutching a heavy book.

'That's enough.' The deadly finality in his tone froze her for just one second, and in that instant he moved so that before she could do anything to escape him he had caught her round the waist and they were both stumbling together. Then she was on the floor.

Effortlessly, he flipped her on to her back, trapping her with his body. He had her hands pinned above her head, his weight holding her down—she could do nothing. She stared up into his eyes—burning blue ice. And her own were like yellow fire.

They were both raging, but just as her anger covered a fear she would not admit to, so there was something else beyond his—she could see it in his eyes. For what seemed like an eternity they stared at each other, both on a knife-edge between hatred and some unknown passion. And then, just when she thought she could bear it no longer, something imperceptible tipped them over the edge.

Caspar's mouth came down hard on hers, and instead of fighting him she was clinging to him as though she could never let him go. He had released her wrists and his arms were round her, crushing her to him, as his tongue invaded every last recess of her mouth as though in his turn he could never have enough of her.

When finally he broke off, they lay together, his cheek against hers, breathing fast. She could feel a heart beating between them, but couldn't tell whose it was. She remembered something Monica had said—it seemed a lifetime ago now—'When you're really in love you're like one person, even though you are two . . . and that is why you fight . . .'

He raised his head to look down at her. The ice she had last seen in his eyes had melted into that deceptive blue under the gold lashes.

'You idiot,' he said unevenly. 'I've been trying to show you since London that you mean one hell of a lot to me. I didn't think I could have made it any more obvious! Why can't you tell me what I mean to you?'

'How much is one hell of a lot?' she whispered, hanging on to the one tiny remaining thread of her former resolve—she wouldn't let the Hugh thing happen all over again.

He began to kiss the side of her face, moving down the hairline, and then along the line of her jaw, while his hand crept up under her jersey, his fingers light and teasing as they travelled across her ribs and under the lace that covered her breast. It was no answer, unless it was the very one she didn't want—that he was prepared to take her as his mistress, no more. But she couldn't fight the heady seductiveness of it any longer.

Then his thumb began a slow circling movement, and as she sensed her nipple peak and harden, she closed her eyes, and a feeling of exquisite delight shot through her body. It was the first time they had shared such intimacies together, and the intensity of her own reaction surprised her into a little gasp.

He was holding her tightly against him, one arm under her back, but he broke off what he was doing, a frown drawing the fair eyebrows together. 'Am I hurting you?'

She looked at him. 'No—why?'

'I've just thrown you on to the floor,' he said, his voice roughened by the desire he was trying to control. 'I thought I might have given you a few bruises. Did I?'

She touched the side of his face with her fingers, and then brushed back the untidy hair. It was thick and fine under her hand. She smiled at him. 'I don't know yet. But I don't mind.'

Despite all her resolutions she was impatient for him to touch her again, her body craving the experience of his far more intimately yet. What they had just done was only a beginning, and she had never before felt such shameless longing.

'Caspar?' she said unevenly.

He was still looking down at her, blue eyes thoughtful. 'What exactly happened with your banker?' The long mouth and determined jaw looked uncompromising now, and she couldn't account for the sudden change of mood.

'Why do you want to know?' she asked shakily. 'I told you—he's got another girlfriend. Someone more suitable . . .'

His mouth quirked briefly. 'You mean to say you weren't suitable? Never! In what way could such a beautiful, lively, impulsive, sweet and passionate woman possibly be unsuitable?' The adjectives had been punctuated by kisses, and he was looking down at her in a way that made it difficult to reply.

'Do you really think I'm all those things?' she asked breathlessly.

'Are you still in love with him?' He ignored her question.

'No.' Her answer was almost a whisper. She wanted to say, I don't think I ever was—it's you I love. But she couldn't, not until he told her what she needed to know about his own feelings. 'Why do you want to know?' Surely now he would tell her he loved her.

'Because if I'm going to make love to you I have to be sure you're not someone else's . . . not in any way.'

It wasn't the assurance she wanted so desperately, and it would be madness to let him go on without the commitment she longed for, but when his lips touched hers again she felt such a surge of desire she could no longer resist him.

She wound her legs round his, impatient of the barriers of clothing between them, and in an instinctive attempt to destroy whatever restraint he had been exercising, wantonly her mouth invited his kiss. With soft, slow movements, he increased their mutual hunger to the point where she broke off with a little cry, her body telling his with each increasingly fevered response of her need for him.

One hand slid lingeringly down over her thigh and up again, and she found herself arching against him, her fingers twisting in his hair as his tongue began that slow circling movement that made her breasts ache under his touch. He was intent on carrying her with him at his own pace into an unfamiliar, compelling world, and all she could do was abandon herself to him utterly.

She was hardly conscious of the sound that broke in upon them but she was aware that Caspar very abruptly stopped what he was doing. He looked up quickly, and then to her amazement rolled swiftly away from her, twitching down her sweater to cover her breasts as he did so. Her body still fired by his, she was astonished by the half-amused, half-embarrassed look he gave her as he pulled her into an upright sitting position. Her back was to the door.

'Bloody hell. Don't you even *knock* when you come into a room?'

The reply, heavily accented with German, was aggrieved. 'But zuh door voz open!'

Bianca turned, dazed by the intensity of interrupted passion, her face flushed and her eyes scarcely focused.

Then she became embarrassingly aware that she was sitting on the floor in a dishevelled state—and only seconds before she had been lying on it, naked from neck to navel, with Caspar on top of her, in an abandonment that she had never known existed.

A young man was in the doorway, tall, thin, with a frizz of brown curls standing up on his head, and a pair of gold-rimmed grandfather's spectacles on his nose.

She turned scarlet at the thought of what he must have witnessed. Then she looked back at Caspar.

'I suppose you mean the door wasn't properly shut,' he said awkwardly. 'Which is not the same thing.' There was something very endearing about his manner, half careless, half embarrassed; it told her as much about him in a few seconds as she had learned in all the hours she had spent with him up to now.

Then he grinned. 'Odd how people have a way of walking in on my most intimate moments—Bianca's done it, too. Bianca, meet Johannes. Bianca's expressed quite an interest in you, Hans, and she thinks as a forger you're asking for everything you get.'

She scrambled to her feet as the tall German stooped to shake hands with her. He wasn't quite her idea of a Hans of German folk-tales, but she liked the gleam of amusement behind the gold-rimmed glasses.

'I have very much wanted to meet you, Bianca. Caspar talks of nobody else!'

Surprised, she glanced across at Caspar; he had a very peculiar expression on his face.

'I can't imagine what you've heard—I hope it wasn't too bad!' she exclaimed nervously.

Johannes laughed. 'Bad? For weeks he rings me up at night—Hans, she is so beautiful—Hans, I am in love viz her . . .'

Astonished, Bianca looked across at Caspar. It was the nearest to acute embarrassment that she was ever going to see. Johannes had jumped to the understandable conclusion that there had been an explanation between them.

'Is this true?' she asked, with a hidden smile. For once she had the chance of turning the tables on him.

Typically, he recovered his composure so fast that she had no time to take advantage of the situation. 'Perfectly true,' he said. 'I do think you're beautiful and sexy. The only thing I'm worried about is your intelligence! I've been telling you just those things since the second day I met you, and you don't seem to have understood a word.'

'. . . I have to meet zis voman, I tell myself,' Johannes was saying. 'He is obsessed and he hasn't even seen her viz her clothes off. She must be quite somesing!'

It was her turn to be embarrassed. 'What on earth have you been telling him?' she demanded accusingly.

'Nothing to what I'm going to tell him, if he doesn't shut up!' Caspar replied. 'Hans, if you can't converse like a civilised forger you'd better go—you've interrupted a very vital discussion, and your contributions to it have been remarkably unhelpful . . .'

'Some discussion!' said his friend cheerfully.

Bianca enjoyed the evening from that point onwards. They ate an impromptu meal cooked by Caspar, who refused, quite rightly, to believe she had eaten anything since that morning, and drank wine. She enjoyed the talk too, characterised by its rapid switches between German, Italian and English, about art and artists and who was selling what to whom.

She also liked Johannes. He had a droll manner, and was a mine of odd information. She had not met a single one of Caspar's friends so far with whom she had not got on well. It made a change from the old days with Hugh.

After a while, giving in to the tiredness that was beginning to catch up with her, she leaned against Caspar. They were together on the sofa and, when he put his arm round her, she rested her head on his shoulder and gave up her part in the conversation. She listened for a while, and then followed a more serious train of thought of her own, inspired by what she had unexpectedly learned of Caspar from his friend's unguarded remarks. He was in love with her—there was no doubt of that now—just what did that amount to exactly?

Finally it was Johannes who talked, launched on an enthusiastic monologue that looked as though it could last the night.

She had no idea how much time had passed when Caspar took a small piece of card from his pocket.

'Johannes,' he said, 'old friend. Here is the address of an excellent café, frequented by Stephen Bates and others at this time of night, and you can talk there till morning. Because,' he went on relentlessly, 'if you stay here any longer, not only are you going to think us rude for ignoring you, but you'll be very embarrassed as well. This time I refuse to be put off.'

The gold-rimmed glasses gleamed, and Johannes gave a good-natured grin.

"All right,' he said, 'one forger knows when he's not wanted—*schlafen Sie!*'

And he made his exit, closing the door ostentatiously behind him.

'What did he say?' Bianca asked, her mind still half following her own thoughts.

'In German? He told us to go to sleep—a very pointed variation on the usual *schlafen Sie gut*—sleep well—he knows I have no intention of sleeping with such a beautiful woman in my arms!'

The departure of Johannes marked a further change in the evening. Just as that all-consuming desire she had felt earlier had faded into a warm, comfortable glow inside her—the glow of her newly discovered love for this talented, unconventional man—so now that comfortable security was fading away. She had had time to think. It would have been so easy to give herself to him, as she would have done only a couple of hours earlier, driven by the powerful need he had created in her; and now the knowledge that he was in love with her added fuel to it. But that would be a fatal mistake.

By his own admission he was not interested in any long-term commitment, and outside marriage she knew that she would always feel insecure. She couldn't afford to make the mistake she had made with Hugh over again—not when this man already meant so much to her. She didn't want to hurt him, but she had to stop him, before he made it more difficult for them both. They couldn't afford any more of his 'discussions' tonight.

'Caspar——'

He was pulling her to her feet. 'I've got something to show you.'

'No, Caspar, I . . . '

He kissed her cheek lightly, and then the end of her nose. 'Come on. It's not a bed—I promise!'

She mustn't let him involve her further—not tonight. 'I want to go back to the hotel,' she said quietly.

He looked at her for a long minute, the blue eyes quizzical. 'OK,' he said at last. 'If that's what you really want.' Then came the familiar sideways quirk to his mouth. 'But first, come into the studio. Only for two minutes?'

She hadn't the heart to refuse. She took his hand and smiled at him instead, overwhelmed suddenly by a wave of tenderness for him. Please don't make me fight you! she thought. I haven't the strength to say no . . .

He turned on the light when they reached the studio. Canvases stood piled round the walls, just as she remembered. There were paints everywhere, and brushes all over the table. A canvas, covered by a cloth, stood on an easel in the middle of the floor. Instantly, she guessed it must be the much-discussed Mrs Brandt, who had played such a significant part in her life just lately.

'Go and have a look at it,' he said, watching her.

Hesitantly, she crossed the floor. Perhaps he hadn't changed it at all . . .

'This one?'

He nodded, an odd smile on his face. Carefully, she removed the covering, and stood back to look.

A young woman sat on a low stool. She had a painting in her hands, and wore dark clothes with an old-fashioned air to them, and a high-necked blouse. Her hair was long, parted in the centre, and falling over one shoulder in long, rippling curls, and her skin was marvellously painted—of a real translucent paleness. Under finely-drawn dark brows her eyes were almost yellow . . .

She was silent for a long time. Then she said, 'When did you do the sketches for this?'

'That day you were looking at my canvases in here. Don't you like it?'

Yes, she liked it; it was a remarkable painting—how could he have remembered her so well?—but its impact was disturbing. This girl, herself, was everything Caspar had once described to her so critically—the clothes, the hair, the pose, all suggested a demure Victoria miss, yet the expression of the sitter, and above all her eyes, depicted a sort of bright energy and passion very much at odds with her outward self. Was that the way he still saw her?

He came to stand behind her, but didn't touch her. '*The last of the Pre-Raphaelites*—a good title for her, don't you think?'

She turned to face him. 'I thought you didn't want to paint me. Why did you? You said I wasn't interesting enough.'

He looked down at her, but she couldn't read his expression. He reached out, and one of those lean artist's fingers traced an invisible line down her forehead, and her nose, and then broke off to outline her lips. 'Oh, you're interesting enough, my darling. You make a beautiful portrait. You should be flattered . . . Don't you recognise a love-gift when you see one?'

Once again, whatever the words they spoke, the real discussions was going on underneath. He was telling her that he was in love with her—but no more. It was now that she had to tell him it wasn't enough, or it would be too late. Yet how could she bring herself to hurt him with a rejection that half of her didn't want to make? She had known this would happen, and it was worse than she had thought.

She searched for the right words, but there were none.

'Well,' he asked gently. 'My yellow-eyed lady—what do you think?' His finger was under her chin, tilting it firmly so that she had to meet his eyes.

Then, without any of the preliminary phrases she had

been searching for, she blurted out, 'Caspar, I won't be your mistress!' She thought she detected a small change in his eyes, but nothing else. There was a dangerous silence.

'Who said anything about a mistress?' he asked carefully.

'You did! You said last time I was here you'd found a new mistress, but she didn't know it yet. I didn't understand then, but it was me, wasn't it?'

'The word mistress was yours, not mine. But it was true—then.' *Now* what was he saying?

'You're getting cross again!' He was laughing, and despite her resistance pulled her into his arms. 'We've had our Monica-style pillow fight for today—anyway, it's too late to start one now. And I don't think somehow you're really angry, are you?'

'Caspar—let me *go!*' He was infuriating. Why did he have to tease her? He must know he was making it impossible for her.

'No,' he said. 'You want to be held. You want to be kissed. And you want to be made love to. And if you're going to ask me a question, why don't you ask the only one you've been interested in all night?'

She stared at him, her eyes like yellow amber. 'If you're so clever and you've known what it was all along, why haven't you given me an answer?'

He was looking at her with that serene expression she now recognised: he was completely sure of himself. 'OK,' he said agreeably. 'You have exactly two minutes in which to hear all the answers you want. After that you'll be in bed with me, and I can guarantee that it won't be answers you're interested in . . . ' He glanced at his watch. 'Starting now. One—yes, I am in love with you—very, very much. Two—since round about the time I saw you draped in Monica's towel. Three—yes, I did keep you in my apartment longer than I needed to because I was so fascinated by you . . . '

He had begun to back her out of the studio. It was like a shuffling dance across the carpet, his movements dictating hers as he took a step forward, one leg between hers as she took a step back to avoid getting tangled with him.

'Four—I decided to change the portrait of our friend
Mrs B. because I fell in love with you, and you were more
important to me than any painting. Five—no, Monica and
I have never gone back to our former relationship. Six—'
they were in the passage that led to the bedroom '—she's
going to marry her macho Italian. He's called Carlo and
she's known him for months. He tried to get into the café
just as you tried to get out. Obviously a case of bad timing
all round. Seven—I came to London because I wanted to
see *you*. The other things weren't important . . . ' They'd
reached the door. She had to stop this! It would be too late
before he ever—if he ever—got to the answer she wanted!

'Caspar—'

'Shut up, Bianca. I haven't finished. Eight—yes, I was
jealous of Hugh. Nine—yes, I do think you're beautiful and
desirable, much more beautiful and desirable than Monica,
and quite unlike any woman I've ever met before . . . ' He
had shut the bedroom door very firmly, but the inexorable
backing process still went on.

'Nine was quite nice—' she said, a little desperately,
'but what's ten?' He gave her a push, and she toppled gently
backwards on to the bed. Then he was on top of her. 'This?'
he said. And very slowly, and very purposefully, he touched
his lips to hers and gave her the longest, gentlest, most
skilfully seductive kiss she'd ever had. He looked down at
her. His hair, as always, was untidy, and he was so dear to
her that it was as though her whole body was filled with
her intolerable heartache.

'I won't be your mistress,' she whispered.

'I'm not asking you to. You were asking the
questions—remember?'

For a moment she wondered what he was doing as he
slid a hand down between them and she could feel his
knuckles somewhere near the top of her thigh. Then he
began to pull something carefully out of his pocket, leaning
a little away from her. She glanced down to see that he was
slowly drawing out a long necklace of silver links . . .

There was something familiar about it. Then she

remembered. It was the one she had seen in the jeweller's shop he had taken her to the first time they had gone out together.

'Caspar! How did you——?'

'I got the jeweller to make this—it's a copy of the one he sold, but definitely not one that's likely to have the police after it!' He took her left hand. 'Spread your fingers,' he instructed. Then, very slowly, he wound it round where Hugh's engagement ring might once have been.

At that moment she was aware of nothing more than a pleased astonishment that he had remembered something so unimportant when they had first met. That was the day she had bought Hugh's cuff-links. She still had them—but they were useless now. She had chosen a man who never did up his shirtsleeves . . . She began to smile: they suddenly summed up for her the difference between the two men—one who was neat and organised and passionless . . . and one who was not. She couldn't comprehend the full measure of her happiness yet; that would come later.

She put her arms round the portrait painter, and kissed him.

'I love you so much,' she said.

Then he kissed her again. It was even better, if that was possible, than the last time, because this time he didn't stop . . .

Now, as they could spark each other to temper, their desire created that familiar mutual hunger that could so quickly consume them both if they let it—and this time there was no reason why it shouldn't. The fires that had been kindled earlier were still smouldering, only waiting to blaze up again, brighter, fiercer, more demanding than before. Impatiently he loosened her clothing, and she arched closer to him, wild for the contact of his body against hers and for that ultimate possession they had been denied for so long. There was no time, or need, for seduction—she was aware only that her desperate ache for him was fully matched by his for her, and that everything he was doing to her increased that hunger even while it fed it. Then she was being swept along on the tide of sensation he was creating in her, so fast, so agonisingly sweet, that she thought she would die of it before he caught her up, shuddering, into some unearthly delight where there was a dazzling peace she had never found before.

They lay together in exhausted silence, and once again she couldn't tell whose heart it was beating between them. She could feel the hectic pulse in his body slowing as he lay with his cheek against hers, his breath fanning her hair. She felt as though she were still floating somewhere in a cloud of happiness, that was made of her love for the wonderful man she was going to marry, and his love for her, and that it was going to take a long time to get back to the real world.

But then he raised his head and looked down at her, smiling. She recognised at once the wicked gleam in his eye.

'I'm sorry,' he said softly. 'I couldn't wait to take your clothes off properly. Have I shocked you?'

She moved languorously under him, enjoying the sensation of the weight of his body on hers, and looked up at him through her lashes. 'No,' she said, knowing that the way she was looking at him was a further invitation. 'Even if I haven't ever made love with most of my clothes on before . . . Why?'

'I didn't mean it to happen so quickly,' he said ruefully.

She laughed, and then murmured against his lips. 'You mean you've got that reputation you were always boasting about to keep up?'

'My reputation was well deserved, I'll have you know! But then I had never met anyone I wanted quite so desperately as I want you.'

'Is that why against all your principles you've decided to marry me?'

He gave her a heart-stopping smile. 'No. I've decided to marry you because I love you.'

'But you haven't even asked me yet!' she said breathlessly.

'No,' he agreed, 'but then I don't need to. It's what you've been asking *me* all evening. I've guessed what the matter was ever since I discovered you were jealous of Monica, but I couldn't be sure. I hoped you'd tell me ... ' He sounded wistful.

'But women don't ask men if they'll marry them!' she protested weakly.

'Don't be so boringly conventional, Mrs Caspar-Reissman-to-be! We wouldn't even be here now if I hadn't decided I couldn't wait any longer ... And I still can't ... ' There was no mistaking the look in his eyes this time.

He started to take off the remains of her clothes, pushing up her jersey and making her laugh when he kissed the sensitive skin of her bare midriff. 'And to think I'm marrying a girl I haven't even seen properly undressed!' he said. 'I seem to remember commenting once before on your remarkable modesty.'

'And I thought I'd never met anyone more conceited!' she teased softly. 'Imagine telling me I was the only woman you'd met who wouldn't take her clothes off in front of you!' She turned her attention, but not very single-mindedly, to the few buttons that were still done up on his shirt.

After a while he asked, 'How soon do you think your mother could fly out here? I've a feeling she'll never forgive me if she doesn't get the chance to come to her only daughter's wedding.'

At the mention of Carla her only daughter gave a conscience-stricken gasp.

'Oh, hell,' she said.

'What?'

'I forgot the paint.'

He began to laugh. 'Do you mean my new Carla James Designer Kitchen is going to have to wait?'

'I could fly home tomorrow and fetch it?' she suggested, with no very convincing attempt at penitence.

'No, you couldn't.'

'Why not?' The question was muffled in the Monica-inspired Italian jersey he was pulling over her head.

He waited until he could look her in the eye. 'Because,' he said slowly, 'earlier on this evening, while Hans was here, just as an insurance policy, I took your passport . . .'

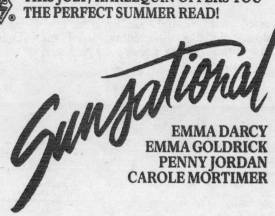